# WAHIDA CLARK PRESENTS

# SWAG

A NOVEL BY

# ANGEL SANTOS

Wahida Clark Presents Publishing
60 Evergreen Place
Suite 904
East Orange, New Jersey 07018
973-678-9982
www.wclarkpublishing.com

Swag by Angel Santos
ISBN 13-digit 978-1936649396
ISBN 10-digit 193664939X

Library of Congress Cataloging-In-Publication Data:
LCCN 2013914911
  1.   Street Lit    2. African American Fiction   3. Urban Fiction

Cover design and layout by Nuance Art.*.
Book design by NuanceArt@wclarkpublishing.com
Proofreader Rosalind Hamilton
Sr. Editor Linda Wilson

# Acknowledgements

First and foremost, all praise is due to the Creator. Thank you for the blessings and the trials. Kaylin, my husband, I knew when I first laid eyes on you that you were the one for me. Thank you for blessing me with our beautiful daughter Jahara. Mommy, I love you no matter what. Thanks for always telling me how proud you are of me.

Ms. Tasha Macklin and your hubby Trae, thank you both for inspiring me to write. Who would have thunk it? ☺ Let's see where this road takes us.

Wahida Clark, you know what it is. Much love and respect always. Uncle Yah Yah. Your books, Uncle Yah Yah parts 1 and 2 has changed my life. Your philosophy is a movement, all within itself.

Treena Burnette, thanks for your support, encouraging words and marketing. You are turning Trae, Tasha and myself into beasts. Love you much.

To the readers, thank you for your continues support. The Wahida Clark Presents brand is all for you.

# Dedication

This book is dedicated to my daddy, brother
and sister. May you all R.I.P.

# PROLOGUE

**"Baby, I swear I don't trust these niggahs,"** she tried to tell her hardheaded man, who waved her off cockily.

"Ma, don't worry. I been doin' this too long to let these nigguhs catch me slippin'," he answered, as he sat on the couch counting money on the coffee table.

She knew her man well enough to know when his mind was made up. It was final. Still, her gut screamed that something was wrong.

After showering, she got out wet because she liked to air dry. She went into the living room and struck a pose.

"You like what you see?"

"He glanced up and smiled. Truly, she was beautiful with coke bottle curves, but he had to stay focused.

"Is that what's for dinner?" he joked.

"It is if you waiting for me to cook," she answered smartly because she hated to cook.

Before he could reply, someone knocked on the door. He stood to answer.

"Give me five, all right?"

Reluctantly, she nodded, her stomach still protesting as she headed for the back of the apartment.

She heard two male voices enter the apartment, voices she would never forget. Voices that would chase her in her dreams. Just as she put on her panties, she heard the series of shots that her stomach had been warning her about. Fear made her want to scream, to run up front, to do *something*, but her survival instincts kicked in. Everything in her acknowledged that her man was dead. But then she heard, "Yo, I swear I heard this niggah talkin' to somebody before he opened the door."

The frightened woman froze when she heard the approaching footsteps.

\* \* \* \* \* \*

The second assassin stepped over the man's twitching body. He paused, looking down through his cold black eyes, sucking in the man's soul. Satisfaction rose in his gut as he headed down the hallway. He checked the bathroom in the hall before entering the master bedroom. He paused in the doorway. Human presence didn't always have to be seen to be felt. It was like electricity that weighted the air. He thought he felt that weight and stepped into the room, gun held high, ready for action. Quickly, he opened the closet door and thrust his gun inside, moving clothes aside with the barrel. He looked around the room, but then glanced at the bed. Just as he started to bend over to look under it, killer number one came to the door.

"Nigguh, what the fuck is you doing? Let's go!"

"Man, I'm telling you the nigguh was talking—"

"Fuck that. We out! I know someone heard all them shots!"

Reluctantly, killer number two left out behind his partner.

\* \* \* \* \* \*

Hiding under the bed felt like lying in a coffin, especially when she saw the pair of Timbs enter the room. She was already holding her breath. But when he came in, she stopped breathing and watched the boots turn toward the closet. Then she watched as they turned toward the bed. She could've reached out and touched them. They were that close. She could feel him looking at the bed, and a serene calm came over her.

In her mind she was prepared to die. So she slowly, quietly, let out her breath, anticipating it to be her last, when suddenly killer number one came in.

The distraught female still didn't believe she'd survive until she heard both sets of footsteps recede and the front door close. She waited a few more moments and then slid from under the bed, trembling with every step of her bare feet as she headed up the hallway.

The sight of her man lying in a pool of his own blood zapped her of strength. She almost passed out. Her knees got so weak she held onto the wall for support, sobbing lightly as she slowly crossed the room and stood over him. One of his eyes was half-open but looked like a lifeless marble. His blood and brains were spread in an uneven pool. She knelt beside him. If she had believed in God she would've prayed, but she had been through too much in her life to believe in anything but her own will.

The money and coke lay on the table untouched.

It hadn't been a robbery. This was a message, and she understood it loud and clear. It was a message she wouldn't forget. She closed his one open eye, kissed his lips, and sang a song in Creole that only he'd understand.

# Chapter One
### *One year later on Mother's Day . . .*

Not the one that comes once a year, but the one that comes once a month on the first and fifteenth, when the hood is flooded with government checks. The block looked like an open market in a Third World Country. Abandoned cars sitting on cinder blocks lined the street. Winos huddled around garbage cans aflame, the fire elongating their shadows grotesquely over vacant lots. Madison Avenue was the hottest block in the city. Money flowed like water.

The scene screamed poverty, but it was also a million dollar block. Dope fiends shuffled back and forth. A young boy herded them like cattle, keeping order.

"Get yo' shit and go! Keep it movin', yo'. Keep it movin'! Spot is hot!"

The block lieutenant, an eighteen year old named Jo-Jo surveyed the scenery proudly. He was on the come up. His name was beginning to ring bells in the street.

Jo-Jo checked his watch, a diamond encrusted Rolex. A quarter to midnight. He was waiting on the bag man to come through and pick up the money and drop another package. Shit was going like water . . . smooth.

"Yo, muthafucka," one of the young boys growled, kicking a bum lying out against a chain link fence. "Get the fuck up!"

The bum lifted his head weakly, started to speak, but vomited instead. The young boy jumped back.

"Yo! What the fuck?" He kicked the bum harder. "You betta not had got none on my shit," he warned, checking his sneakers under the streetlight.

Jo-Jo laughed.

"Yo, B. Chill. Old muthafucka already 'bout to die, yo!"

"He betta hurry up and do it," the young boy replied.

Jo-Jo started to say something, but a dark blue hooptie cut the corner. It was the drop.

"Yo, yo, heads up, stay up!" Jo-Jo shouted, making sure his team was on point, keeping their eyes open for anything shady.

The team spread out, triggers pointed, cocked, locked and loaded, heads on swivel. When they were in place, Jo-Jo whistled, and looked up to the window behind him. Someone dropped a duffle bag out the window. Jo-Jo caught it by the handle. The hooptie stopped in the middle of the street. Jo-Jo started toward it. His team had the perimeter secure, but they didn't know the enemy was already in their midst. They didn't pay attention to the bum whose eyes weren't bloodshot or clouded. They were clear and focused. The bum rose up, cradling an AK-47 with a modified firing pin and banana clip—in other words, a fully automatic chopper.

They never saw it coming.

The AK stuttered and spit fire, blowing out the young boy's back that had kicked him, and bursting Jo-Jo's skull into a rain of blood, bones, and gray matter under the shine of the streetlight. The team was taken by surprise. It took them a second to locate the direction of the shots and fire back, a precious second that cost another young boy his life.

The bag man tried to pull off. The bum, with deadly aim, fired a quick burst and blew the driver's brains all over the windshield. The car rolled into a parked car.

The rest of the team fired wildly, like thugs with their adrenaline flowing. They just squeezed and shot, no aim, no method. The bum grabbed the duffle bag out of Jo-Jo's dead hand. As he rose up, a single shot whizzed through the air and hit the bum dead in the chest, throwing him on his back.

"Fuck!" the bum barked through gritted teeth.

The wind had been knocked out of him. A lot more would've been knocked out of him had he not had on a bulletproof vest. He rose up firing, only missing the rest of the team because they ducked and took cover. It gave him enough time to sprint across the street to the hooptie. Shots flashed around him as he snatched the dead driver out the car, tossed the bag in the passenger seat, and jumped in. He stayed low as he floored the car, metal grinding against metal as he scraped up against the car the bag man had hit.

The back window exploded, shattering into pieces as the young boys came out of hiding like roaches. He screeched off and sped away from the scene.

The bum snatched off the rags he was wearing, stripping down to the bulletproof vest. His adrenaline had his heartbeat pounding so loud he couldn't hear the tiny voice screaming, "Yo! What the fuck? Tee!"

He scowled. *Sounds like a phone.* As he looked around he spotted a phone wedged under the duffle bag. He picked it up.

"Yo, Tee! What—"

"This ain't Tee." He chuckled.

"Who this? Yo, somebody tell me what's going on now!" the voice barked with authority.

He laughed.

# S W A G

"What's going on? I got the money . . . and I got the yayo," he taunted, using the line from Scarface.

The voice went silent, but then said, "Chump change, you bitch ass nigga. But you still a dead man!"

The telegraphed threat made him laugh. He tossed the phone out of the window and watched it smash in the rearview.

# Chapter Two
### *Another scorcher . . .*

T he ghetto was red hot, frying fewer than 100-degrees-plus temperatures for the eighth day in a row. Power outages broke out in several parts of the city, tempers and the murder rate had jumped. The city was on fire.

Officer Jazmine Coleman tipped back her motorcycle police helmet and wiped the sweat off her brow. She was steaming in more ways than one. The mirror shades were the only thing keeping the world from seeing the fire in her eyes. Underneath her uniform and her bulletproof vest, her whole body was drenched in sweat.

She had only been out of the Police Academy a little over a month, and she was stuck giving out parking tickets. This definitely wasn't why she joined the force. She had plans, big plans, but she couldn't make a move until she got a break.

Today was her lucky day. But at the moment she definitely didn't feel lucky. At the moment, she was in the process of giving a ticket to a young Asian dude in a brand new BMW.

He was pleading, but starting to get belligerent. She was aggravated and ready to go postal, when a green Toyota Camry shot through the intersection with a police car in hot pursuit. She heard the call over her radio:

*Dispatch, this is 94. We're in pursuit of a green Toyota Camry, license, David-Paul-Alpha 3-6-1. Heading West on—correction, the suspect just made a left heading North on*

# S W A G

*Turner Boulevard. Request immediate assistance. Suspect could be armed.*

That's all she needed to hear. In the rush to get on her motorcycle, she handed her ticket pad and pen to the Asian dude and roared off to join the chase.

Jazmine had been waiting for a moment like this to prove her worth. To make her big career move, she knew she had to have a stand out moment, so she was determined to make this that moment. She pushed the bike, dipping through traffic in hot pursuit of the chase. She spotted the Camry. A dude was driving and a girl was in the passenger seat. Two more cruisers had responded to the call. The Camry driver definitely knew what he was doing, whipping and dipping the vehicle like a pro. His only mistake was when he came to the next intersection. He should've dipped instead of whipped. He sideswiped a delivery van and ran up on the curb. Without missing a beat, he jumped out and kept it hot on foot, sprinting off like he was possessed by the spirit of Jesse Owens.

By the time Jazmine joined the foot race a few seconds later, two other officers were in pursuit. She shot past them like they were standing still. Jazmine didn't have runner's thighs for nothing. Even though he had a head start, she was in top shape and had a natural speed that put her on pace with the dude.

The dude saw her closing in. He turned abruptly to his left and hopped a five-foot chain link high fence, using his hands to vault him over. This cost him some time because Jasmine used a car parked beside the fence. She hit the trunk and then leaped the fence, landing in stride. The dude cut through an alleyway and disappeared inside an abandoned warehouse. Jazmine pulled her gun as she surveyed the situation. She had looked the dude over as he ran. He wasn't armed, but he had a healthy build. If he ambushed her and gained the upper hand . . .

She started to wait for back up, but her quick mind came up with a better idea.

"Car 94, come in 94," she hoarsely whispered into her walkie-talkie on her shoulder.

"Go ahead, Car 94."

She moved cautiously through the door.

"Do you have the girl in the car in custody?"

"Affirmative."

"In *thirty* seconds have her call this dude. *Thirty* seconds, 10-4?"

"Ten-four."

Jazmine trained the gun in front of her, stepping stride over stride, her every sense turned up to the max. The warehouse was one big cavernous room. Barrels and crates littered the room. There was no other way out.

A large rat screeched and scurried away, making Jazmine bristle. Her nerves were tighter than a guitar string. In her mind she tried to keep a count, but when she got to twenty-eight, she heard the phone ring off to her right. Jazmine spun and fired off several shots in that direction, but purposely high.

"Hol'hol'hol'. Gotdamn, hol' up! Don't shoot!" the dude squawked.

"Then come out *slow!*" she demanded.

The dude came out from a stack of crates with his hands up.

"On your face, *now* . . . Slow! Don't fuck up! If I make a mistake, you won't know about the apology!"

Ai'ight, man!"

The dude got down on his face, spread eagle. Jazmine approached. The dude turned his head, looked at her, and rolled his eyes.

"Goddamn! How the fuck you caught by a bitch?" he hissed.

She put her knee in his back and yanked his arms behind him, just as three more officers ran in.

"Just make sure you smile when you say that," she retorted, and then put the cuffs on extra tight.

* * * * * *

By the time she got back to the precinct, the story of the quick thinking traffic cop had beat her back. Especially since the dude had three kilos of cocaine in the car.

When she walked in, all eyes were on her and not just because of her heroics. Once she took off her motorcycle helmet and sunglasses, all eyes stayed on her. From her full pouty lips to her kewpie doll nose, short, spiked hair, and cattish eyes, her resemblance to Sanaa Lathan was unmistakable and tantalizing, and her strut said she knew it. In the short time she had been a cop, half the force had hit on her, and not all were men. But she brushed them all off like lint because she had a plan, and it all began with Detective Hall.

Hall was the chief detective of the Narcotics Division. Narcotics was the fast track to rapid advancement up the cop ladder and beyond. Hall didn't like slackers, because he ran a tight ship. But with her big arrest she knew she'd be on his radar, and she would definitely make the most of the opportunity.

By any means necessary.

She caught sight of Hall and a junior detective heading toward his office.

"Detective Hall," she called out as she approached.

Hall stopped and looked back, watching her approach. His eyes appraising her. He was a short bull of a black man with a preference for impatience.

"Well, if it ain't Robo Cop," he gruffed with a chuckle as Jazmine caught up.

"News travels fast around here," she replied.

"That, and I keep my ear to the ground."

The junior detective branched off as Hall reached his office. Jazmine paused at the door.

"Umm, Detective Hall, if I could . . ." She let her voice trail off, in a questioning manner.

"Whatever it is, just make it quick," he answered, plopping down behind his desk.

She entered and closed the door.

"That, uhh, incident from earlier you referred to . . . That's what I wanted to talk to you about," she began.

"What about it?" he retorted, looking over a folder on his desk.

"I've been on the force for over a month, and since I've been here, I've been assigned to the traffic division. And while traffic law is . . . important, I really think I'd be more of an asset in narcotics."

He glanced up with an amused expression.

"Oh, you do, do ya?"

"Yes, sir. I really do. I know those streets, sir. But I joined the force to put that knowledge to good use. I'm quick on my feet, sir. I'm just asking for a chance!"

Hall leaned back in his chair, took off his glasses, and placed them on the table. "Officer . . ."

"I'm sorry, sir. Officer Jazmine Coleman."

"Coleman. Where you from, Coleman? I detect a drawl in your voice."

She smiled. "Georgia, sir."

"Georgia . . . and you come to the big city to put your knowledge to use, huh? Now, I'll give you that you're quick on your feet. That phone thing was quick thinking. But you know what I think, Officer Coleman."

Jazmine shielded herself for criticism.

"What do you think, sir?"

"I think you're a renegade . . . a cowgirl, which in my book is a problem waiting to happen. You may've nabbed a good collar, but you were assigned to *write tickets*. You didn't do your job. Now, I admire ambition. Hell, I don't trust a sumbitch unless he has some, but there's a right way and a wrong way to go about it," he told her. Then he put his glasses back on, leaned back over the folder, and added, "Now, do that well enough, then come and talk to me."

Jazmine stood there a moment, looking at his bowed head. She turned to the door, but instead of opening it, she simply closed the blinds. When Hall glanced up, he remarked, "So, now what you gonna do? Beat me up?"

Jazmine ignored his quip, rounded the corner of his desk with a slow strut, and then sat one cheek of her shapely ass on the desk.

"Detective, I know you're after a guy named Terrance Love and his crew, but you can't arrest him. It's all over the department, and it's no secret that you're none too happy with your people for not getting him . . . I can get him. Where four men fail, send in one woman. She'll get the job done. Nobody knows me. They don't know my face. I haven't been around long enough. I'm perfect for an undercover," she propositioned him, never losing eye contact. Putting extra sexy syrup on her drawl, she added, "And I'm willing to do whatever it takes to convince you so."

Hall chuckled.

"Wow, Georgia, you've got a pretty big set of peaches on you. Don't you know I can have you suspended for sexual harassment for this?"

Jazmine shrugged. "That's only if you feel harassed. Do you feel harassed, detective? You think I don't know about the pool going around, betting on who's gonna screw the new girl?" She smiled and winked. "How much you in for, detective?

Hall smirked at the reference to the pool. Almost every man at the precinct wanted to fuck Jazmine. He couldn't deny her sexuality, nor could he help but admire her unabated ambition. She was starting to look like an offer he couldn't refuse.

"Ambitious," he remarked, looking her over.

"Vivacious," she replied with a smirk.

"Well, you know . . . I was just going to go home and pop a couple of burgers in the microwave."

"I make a helluva Alfredo."

". . . And maybe watch the game—"

"I love basketball."

"And then"—he began eyeing her steadily—"go to bed."

Jazmine smiled. "I never wear panties."

His dick jumped in his pants just from the thought.

"If you were to . . . drop by . . . I won't throw you out," he signified.

The look between them said the deal was sealed.

* * * * * *

"Ohhh, yesss, daddy. Mmmm, right there, right . . . there!" Jazmine squealed with total abandon as she rode Hall's dick at a feverish pace.

Instead of fucking her, she was fucking him as he gripped her hips just to hold on. Her pussy was so wet, every stroke sounded like wet, hungry lips smacking together.

As an older man, his secret of his success was the little blue pill, but he couldn't hold out much longer. The pussy was toe-curling scrumptious. He gripped her hips and flipped her over on her back, legs pinned back, and he pounded her vigorously.

"Yeah, daddy, beat this pussy," she growled, biting her bottom lip.

He obliged her, but it wasn't long before he came hard deep inside of her, and she squealed her way to her own explosion.

Exhausted, Hall collapsed on top of her. Jazmine giggled and caressed his ear.

"After all that, I'm through with young men."

Hall, catching his breath, chuckled as he rolled over to his back.

"You know, you may be a natural undercover."

"What you mean?"

He looked at her with an amused expression.

"Because you're a helluva actress."

They both laughed. Jazmine cuddled up next to him, reaching down and squeezing his dick.

"Don't underestimate yourself," she purred, kissing his neck.

Hall took her hand off his dick.

"You gonna have to give me a minute. The blue pill ain't *that* good."

Jazmine sat up with her legs curled under her, leaning her weight on her right arm.

Hall eyed her admiringly. She was beautiful. The type of woman that he knew couldn't be possessed. But her choice of profession intrigued him.

"You know, you're almost too pretty to be a cop," he remarked.

She smiled her thanks.

"It kinda runs in my family, that and the military. My father raised me more like a drill sergeant than a daddy," she joked, but in her eyes, Hall detected a touch of pain. He didn't try to push it. Instead, he changed the subject.

"If you would've waited, you wouldn't have had to go through all this."

Jazmine shrugged.

"It's just sex, no big deal. Besides, you needed me."

"Oh, *I* needed *you*?" he replied.

"Exactly! Because, you won't get Love without me," she answered confidently.

Just hearing the name soured his mood. Of all his years on the force, he had never seen a crew so tight, airtight and Teflon. Nothing got in and nothing stuck.

"Love is a murderer, a drug dealing lowlife with nine hundred lives. What makes you think you can get him when I couldn't?" Hall gruffed.

Jazmine smiled.

"Because you tried to go get him, but I'm gonna bring him to you."

"With what? That?" he asked, nodding to her fat-lipped pussy.

She pointed to her head.

"Naw . . . with this."

# Chapter Three

*Across town a few hours later . . .*

Antman came out of a motel room at the Days Inn with one of the jump-offs under his arm. Her name was Michelle, and she reminded him of Nicki Minaj, short, thick, and juicy. They walked toward the cab that awaited them. Antman knew how to creep. He left his car parked at the bar and took a cab to the jump-off. He had to keep up appearances for his wife.

"Baby, I told you. Now, don't act like that. I *need* to go shoppin'," Michelle whined as they got in the cab.

Antman closed the door behind him and sucked his teeth.

"I got you, yo. Ai'ight?"

"That's what you said last time." She pouted.

"Well, then you'll never be broke," he quipped.

"Where to go?" the cabby asked.

"Grove Street, yo," Antman told him as his phone rang. He answered, "Yo . . . Thump, what up . . . Yeah, yeah, no doubt . . . Like a half-hour . . . Yep," he spoke quickly and then hung up.

As they rode, Ant turned to Michelle and said, "Please! Don't you fuck wit' that nigga from out Southside? Why the fuck you ain't ask him?"

Michelle rolled her neck with sass, answering, "'Cause I'm asking you, that's why! Don't even go there wit' me, Ant. For real!"

Amused, he let it go. They arrived on Grove Street.

"Where at, bra?" the cabby asked.

Ant didn't want him to pull up in front of the bar, so he stopped him a block away.

"Right here, yo. I'm good," Ant told him.

The cabby pulled over. Ant went in his pocket and pulled out a knot of hundreds.

"You got change, playboy?" Ant asked.

"Yeah."

Ant put the money in the money cup cut into the Plexiglas separator. When he pushed it closed the cup fell out on the other side in the front seat, broken.

Ant peered over the seat.

"Ay yo, my bad. That shit musta been broke."

"No problem."

Ant had looked down at the money for a second, but when he looked back up, the cabby had a .38 snub pointed through the hole where the money cup used to be.

"Ay—" was all Ant got out, before a single shot caught him in the throat and slammed his body back against the seat.

Michelle stifled her scream.

The cabby got out casually, walked around the car and opened Ant's door. Ant held his throat, blood gushed through his fingers while he gasped for air. He looked up at the cabby with pleading eyes. The cabby looked back through unforgiving ones. He grabbed Ant by the collar and then shot him twice more in the head, point blank, coating the seat behind him with his dying thoughts.

Michelle was hyperventilating.

"Swag! I-I didn't know you were gonna do it right here!" She gasped, looking around frantically to see if anyone was looking.

They were in the residential section of Grove Street. Swag bent over, hands rested on his knees and looked at her. "Chill, okay? We good, okay? We good. Just chill," Swag said in his soothing but raspy baritone.

She nodded but couldn't speak. She reached for the door handle.

"Naw, don't get out. You good right there," Swag told her, raising the gun and shooting her in the face. Blood splattered all over the window as she slumped over on Ant.

Swag, taking his time, took Ant's 40-inch platinum chain off his neck, his diamond watch, the knot of hundreds, and his cell phone. He closed the door, leaving the cab running and walked away. Swag hit the dial button on Ant's cell twice, redialing the last number.

"Yo, you there already?" Thump answered with a question.

"We meet again, huh?" Swag quipped.

"We?" Thump scowled, and then the voice instantly registered. "Ay, yo, who this?"

Swag laughed. "Your man from the other night!"

"Where the fuck is Ant?"

"Sleep. But dig, before you get into that gangsta shit, *don't*! Just know this: If I don't eat, y'all don't eat, period. You wanna holler, you know the number," Swag explained, and then deadened the connection without a reply.

* * * * * *

"Hello! Hello! Hello!" Thump bellowed, holding the phone in front of his mouth and screaming into it.

He was so hot he flung the phone into the wall and watched it smash.

"Yo. Thump, what up? Yo, Thump. Thump! What up?" one of his lackey's asked.

They were in one of the crew's safe houses. Two dudes held the door down with fully automatic AR-15's outside. Three more secured the perimeter. Inside, the sound of the two money machines filled the air.

"Yo, turn them shits the fuck *off*!" Thump barked.

The money machines fell quiet instantly. Thump paced the floor and his team stayed out of his way. He was a big dude. Big, black, and ugly. He looked like the rapper Rick Ross without the beard and one cockeye. They called him Thump because when he hit a nigga, that was all you heard when he hit the floor.

"Yo, I'm tellin' you right now! Right. The. Fuck . . . *now.* Somebody in this room is a dead bitch ass nigguh. That's my word!"

The whole room froze with various degrees of chills up their spine. They looked from one to another.

"Yo, Thump. I'm sayin', what's up, big homie?" one of his braver goons asked.

Thump got in his grill, poking him in the chest to punctuate his every word.

"You don't know? Then you didn't need to know, 'cause if you knew then you fucked up!"

Thump surveyed the room slowly, from face to face. Deep in his heart, he knew somebody in the room had set Ant up. This was the second time in the last month they'd been hit. He knew nobody would even attempt to move on their crew without an inside man guiding their steps. The streets knew how Love's crew got down. Maybe they had forgotten, but Thump was definitely going to remind them.

He dropped his head and pinched the bridge of his nose. That was his moment of silence for his right hand, Antman.

"My word, my nigguh. My *word*," he mumbled, vowing to his now dead homie.

He looked up.

"Ai'ight . . . turn 'em back on," he ordered.

Several seconds later, the splat-a-rat of the bills being counted began again as Thump headed for the door to break the news to Love.

# Chapter Four

Y ou okay?"
As soon as Jazmine walked into his office, he could
tell something was wrong.

Closing the door behind her, she replied, "Yeah . . . Yeah, I am just coming from Homicide. A girl from my complex was found dead in a cab the other night."

"Yeah, I heard. Did you know her?"

"In passing. She lived like two doors down. I don't know . . . just kinda . . . personal when it hits that close to home. Reminds me of a lot of things I'd rather forget," she replied, sitting down in the chair in front of his desk.

Hall could see the moment was wearing on her. She had that look on her face like the night she mentioned her father. He cleared his throat.

"I'm sorry to say, but that's kinda where I wanted to start this briefing."

"Go 'head. I'm good."

Hall handed her a glossy of Antman dead in the back of the cab, and a glossy of his mug shot.

"That's the guy she was killed with, not to mention the cabby we found dead in the trunk of the cab they were killed in.

"A hit," she surmised.

"Exactly. But who gave the nod? The guy's name was Anton Collins aka Antman. He was a ranking member of Love's crew because he was Thump's right hand man."

"Who's Thump?"

Hall reached down and brought up a corkboard. On it were various mug shots and camera shots of Love's crew in a pyramid pattern. He leaned the board against the wall.

"What is that? Your *Love's* family portrait?" she quipped.

He chuckled.

"Yeah, a family of dope pushers, killers, and convicts. Now pay attention. This is Deon Stokes aka Thump." Hall pointed to a picture of Thump that was right under Love's picture at the top. "He's the second in command, the COO to Love's CEO, basically. He makes sure shit rolls downhill. Now *this . . . used to be Ant," Hall remarked, taking down the pictures that were thumbtacked to the board, and replaced it with the picture of Ant, dead and bloody.

She noticed another two pictures at the bottom. One of the dude Jo-Jo, and another equally dead lowly block lieutenant.

"Who are the two dead guys at the bottom?"

Hall shrugged.

"Two dead guys at the bottom literally. Block lieutenants of two very lucrative blocks," he answered and then tapped Love's picture. "And this . . . is Love."

The picture was apparently taken in the club, using a police trick too many people fell victim to when they took pictures. They didn't make the camera man erase it out of the camera. Therefore, police often ended up with extra prints.

Love was standing between two Spanish chicks, dressed in his grown and gangster shit and looking like the model Tyson Beckford.

"Hmmm, he's a cutie," Jazmine remarked.

"Glad you think so," Hall grunted, slightly jealous.

"Well, it looks to me like either an internal power play or a new crew's moving in."

"My money's on the power play angle, because Love's got his claws dug so deep in this city, a crew would have to be suicidal to move in," Hall countered.

"Remember, it's a recession. Hunger makes people crazy."

"And it's getting worse. Love's beginning to get into politics, throwin' his money at a recent city council election. Once that cement dries . . ." He shook his head, and then added, "We gotta stop this cock sucka."

"I concur."

"Okay, Ms. Lady," Hall stated, after sitting down at his desk and folding his hands, "you've got your chance. What are you going to do with it?"

Jazmine looked at the pyramid of pictures for a moment. "I really don't think it's internal. I mean, why kill two nobody block lieutenants? They're pawns. You only do that when you want to destabilize the foundation. You don't burn the house down if you want to take it over. To me, it looks like we're not the only ones trying to take Love down," Jazmine summed up.

Hall nodded as he contemplated her assessment.

"Makes sense, but it adds an x to this equation."

"Which is?"

"If there's a war about to jump off, I don't want to send you into the middle of it."

"Trust me, detective. I'm a big girl. I'll be okay."

He pointed at her.

"Listen here, Georgia. This won't be none of your cowboy shit. You clear *everything* by me. You make one unauthorized move. I'll have you doing high school security, we clear?"

"Yes sir," she replied with a playful salute. "Only one question?"

"What?"

"When do we go shopping? I need an undercover wardrobe." She winked.

# Chapter Five

L ove rode shotgun on his golf cart, while Councilman James Joyner drove over the lush greens of The Spring Ferry Golf Course.

"Councilman, I'm throwing a lot of money at this campaign for one thing, results. I know the game, and I know you know how to play it, bottom line. I got two mentoring programs, and I want some of that federal grant money to go to them. *Period*," Love emphasized smoothly, because it was never necessary for him to raise his voice.

The Councilman, a middle-aged black man with an afro like sports reporter, Steven A. Smith, shifted uneasily in his seat. He was beginning to regret getting in bed with gangsters.

"Mr. Love, things just aren't that simple. I'm—"

"Sure they are."

"Only one vote of a nine man council. Horse trading can only go so far," Joyner complained.

He stopped the cart by the parking lot. Love smiled and patted him on the back.

"That's why I voted for you, Councilman, because I know you're the man for the job."

Joyner started to protest, but Love was already walking away. Love had no doubt he'd get what he wanted, because he always got what he wanted. His success had spoiled him. Not that it had been easy, but neither had he. Love chirped the alarm on his metallic gray BMW 6 series Gran Coupe, taking off his suit jacket as he got in and laid it across the passenger seat.

As he drove, his mind flickered over the conversation with Councilman Joyner. He knew Joyner would come through. It would probably cost him the ability to allocate some of the money to his business partner's construction company. But that was minor to the overall picture. It was the same way in the streets.

It was all thug politics.

The thought made his mind turn to Antman's murder. He understood Thump's point that somebody in the crew was sour, but it didn't add up. Not when they found out that the money Ant was holding, over eight hundred thousand, was still safe in Ant's stash. An inside job would've focused on the money. This was deeper, especially considering the nigga who killed Antman, whom Jo-Jo and Bam reported as having said, "If I don't eat, y'all don't eat."

Just thinking about that made his blood boil. *Dude really thought he could extort a Don?* Love thought. It had been a while since Love had to put his murder game down. He had come up from a youngin', making his presence felt. From a runner to block hugger, and then a lieutenant to having his own block, virtually running the city. There was no way one man was going to be a problem. If he had to scorch the city just to get his man, he would, because he believed in killing mosquitoes with axes.

He stopped at the light. His consciousness surfaced from thoughts long enough to know that Drake was on. He hated Drake. Love leaned over to change the station, and all of a sudden, he felt a strong impact and the whole car shook. He started to go for the gun in the stash, but as he came up looking in the rearview, he saw he had been rear ended by a woman driver. His instincts said 'be easy', as he assessed the situation. Love's adrenaline slowed as he fully realized it wasn't a set up. It was just a fender bender.

He got out the car to assess the damages. The woman still hadn't gotten out of her bronze Honda Accord. She was too busy arguing on her cell phone. Love reached in and blew his horn in an aggravated way to get her attention. He was vexed that his car was fucked up, but looking at a cinnamon complexioned, doe-eyed beauty with full pouty lips that reminded him of Sanaa Lathan, he couldn't stay mad for long.

The woman looked up when he blew his horn and grilled him like he was interrupting. She got out screaming, "Now look what you made me do! I done crashed my shit, nigguh! What! Nigguh, fuck you! How 'bout that. *Fuck —you*, you no-dick-havin', broke-back, bitch ass nigguh! Fuck you!" she spazzed over the phone, even though no one was really on the other end. Then she slammed her phone on the floor of her car with a grunt like Serena Williams serving Ace.

Love watched her with a smirk on his face. She definitely had fire. He liked that. In her heels, she was over six-feet tall and looked to come up to his shoulder, very shapely in statuesque. She filled out her jeans like a stallion, and he could see she wore no bra under her white wife beater, because her cantaloupe-sized breasts jiggled freely with her tantrumized movements.

After she slammed the phone, she finally turned to Love, looked him up and down, and then snapped, "What!"

"What?" he echoed with assured aggravation. "You hit my shit!"

She looked at him, and then at the car.

"That's you?"

"Yeah," he replied like, Duh!

"A BMW? Psst, you can afford it," she remarked dismissively.

Sexy stallion or not, she was pushing a little too much attitude.

He pinched the bridge of his nose like, "Yo man, you got some insurance?"

She took a deep breath. "I'm sorry, I shouldn't have said that. I'm just havin' a bad day. Really, I apologize," she replied in her syrupy southern drawl, pouring it all over him like he was a biscuit, or she was the glaze, and he was the donut.

Something about a southern accent softened people, made the con that much easier because no one believed a southerner could take them fast. Love softened like, "Ma, don't worry about it. Let's just speed this up 'cause we blockin' traffic."

"Oh, I'm sorry." She glanced around, seeing the cars going slowly around them and some drivers rubbernecking. "Let me get my insurance card."

Love walked over as she sat in the driver's seat, started to reach for the glove compartment, but then sat back up.

"Okay. For real, for real, I don't have insurance," she admitted, biting her bottom lip, giving him her cute I-fucked-up *I Love Lucy* look. "I just moved up here from Georgia because I met this guy on Facebook, and he was so cool and I was tired of Georgia. I feel so stupid, but I really needed a change and as soon as—"

Her rapid-fire delivery of run-on sentences jumbled in Love's head just like she knew they would. He held up his hand.

"Yo, relax. Don't stress it."

"No really, I'ma pay for the damages as soon as I get a job."

Love glanced at his watch.

"Look . . . This what we gonna do. You gonna take me to lunch, and we'll call it even."

"Lunch?"

"Lunch, and you payin'." He chuckled.

"Shit, then we must be goin' to McDonald's."

He laughed because her accent made it funny, but that's exactly where they went.

She doubled up the trays and carried their order to the table. As she sat down, she slid him a tray and they divvied the order. He took one of her fries. She smacked his hand. He ate it anyway.

"So, you gonna tell me your name, Country Girl?" He smirked.

"Are you, City Boy?" she shot back.

"I'm Love."

"Love? What you? A stripper or somethin'?"

He laughed.

"Naw ma, that's my last name."

"Oh!" she replied, giving him an approving look that she knew would encourage him. "I'm Jazmine."

"Like the flower, huh?"

She smiled.

"Yeah, like the flower. And . . . I really am sorry. I'm gonna pay for it, I promise."

He ate his fries.

"So you lookin' for a job, huh?"

"Depends on the job," she retorted, skeptically.

"Be easy, ma. You ain't gotta give me that type of look."

"You ain't gotta give me that kind of line."

She may've been country, but Love knew she wasn't green.

"I'm sayin', I got this mentoring agency, and I'ma need a receptionist," he explained.

"Mentoring Agency?"

"Yeah."

"No offense, but you don't look like the . . . mentorin' type," she quipped.

"Never judge a book by its cover."

"Some covers are just easy to read," she shot back.

Love sipped his milkshake and eyed her.

"Yo, ma. I like your style. For real, you seem like somebody I need to know."

"Maybe. But if you do give me a job, it's only one problem."

"Which is?"

"I don't mix business with pleasure." She winked.

"Okay, you're fired." He grinned.

She was in.

Game begins . . .

# Chapter Six

T he sounds of a hot Dirty South hip-hop classic filled the strip club as Swag lounged in the booth in the back in the dark, playing the cut. He wasn't drinking, although several untouched drinks surrounded him. He never drank when he worked, and he was definitely working. He watched a group of ballers across the room, popping bottles and upping the price of pussy with every downpour and drizzle. They were one of Love's out of town crews in town to pick-up and bounce. That was their monthly routine. Routine is a gangsta's enemy. Swag devoured routine.

As the night wore on, they got drunker and Swagger got hungrier. This would be easy money. His thoughts were interrupted by a sweet, and T-Boz-like, sultry voice.

"Waitin' for me, daddy?"

Swag reluctantly tore his eyes away from his marks and onto the face of an angel, with the body of a goddess. Swag looked her over inch by inch, starting at her perfect French pedicure, clearly visible through her see-thru fuck-me-pumps. The arch of the spiked heel had her toned calves looking taunt, tight, and right. Her shapely thighs blossomed into 38-inch hips and a 40-inch ass that swallowed her fire red thong. Swag's eyes traveled up her flat stomach to her pert, juicy, and bare titties that set up firm like they were fake, but they weren't. Her chinky brown eyes sparkled, and her sexy suckable lips shined from the gloss. Her hair was cut short like Kelis and dyed blue. This whole heavenly package was covered in a chocolate, smooth, and blemish free face. She glowed like the moon dipped in Hershey's.

The sweetest thang . . .

She was the type of woman no man could say no to, and her smirk said she knew it. Aggravated for being interrupted, but letting it go because she was a pleasant distraction, Swag just smirked and replied, "Naw, ma. I'm good."

The sexy vixen lifted her right leg slowly, like she was mounting a horse. When she straddled him and sat on his lap, she felt his firm dick lying against his thigh and the feeling made her pussy jump. She was hooked the moment she laid eyes on him. His thuggish demeanor was contrasted by fine features, too fine . . . El-DeBarge fine, with a softness to his roughness expressed through his long eyelashes and his Prince-like aura of androgyny. His short, wavy hair spun 360 degrees with thick waves and his mustache and goatee were shaped up perfectly. Just looking at him made her want to . . .

She started grinding her hips slowly. Swag smiled.

"Ma, I said I'm good."

"Yeah, but good at what? That's what I'm trying to find out," she purred. "I'm Candy Rain. You wanna taste?"

She slid her finger in her thong, pinched her clit, letting out a whimper. Then she stuck the finger in her mouth. "Mm mm, melts in your mouth."

Swag started to answer, but his attention was taken by the movement at his target's table. They were leaving. Everything in him wanted to shove her to the ground and make his move, but he knew she'd remember his face if anything happened.

Inside, Swag shrugged. There would be another chance. Now that he was off duty, Swag picked up one of the untouched drinks, took a sip and eyed Candy. Since he had to cancel his last bitch, he figured Candy would be a good replacement.

By the time his attention was back on her, she was grinding harder, trying to make his dick harder, but it simply stayed firm. She saw he had excellent discipline, but she didn't.

"Sssss, goddamn, daddy. What you do to me?" she groaned, hypnotized by the gaze of his green eyes.

Swag set his drink down, stuck two fingers in it, then slid those same two fingers inside her thong, pulling the hood of her clit back, then massaging and pulling it expertly. Candy put her leg against the wall and grinded it harder. That's all it took to make her cum. She trembled, her shoulders jerked like she was shivering.

"You know you dead wrong for that, right?"

They both laughed softly. Swag swirled the same two fingers in his drink, flicked off the excess, and then downed the drink.

"What's your name, daddy?"

"Swag."

"Mmm, yes you are, but I'm Swag too."

"Oh yeah?"

"You lookin' at me, ain't you? You a new face."

Swag shrugged.

"I'm just passin' through."

She inadvertently placed her hand on his chest and felt his vest under his shirt.

"Expectin' trouble?"

"Naw, but I'd rather be caught wit' it than without it," Swag replied. "I live a hectic life, yo."

"I can see your future, daddy. Take me wit' you," she purred, biting her bottom lip seductively.

"That depends."

"On?"

"On whether you content with bein' a bad bitch, or you wanna be a boss bitch?" Swag cracked.

"I'm already a boss—"

Swag put his finger to her lip to silence her.

"Naw ma, you just for the course. Fuckin' wit' dead end nigguhs doing dead end things. A boss bitch owns the club. She don't dance in it," Swag smoothly crooned, laying out his meaning.

Rain looked at him inquisitively. She liked the way he talked. Most dudes just wanted to fuck. None showed any interest in pouring her a drink.

"I'm all ears, daddy."

He slapped her on the ass.

"Then get the hell up and go get that gwop. These nigguh's giving it away." He smirked. "I'll be waiting when you get off."

When the club closed, true to his word, Swag was sitting on his all black Kawasaki 900 motorcycle when Rain stepped out the door. She hopped on and he pulled off.

Candy lived on the second floor of a three-story home with her mother and son. Swag pulled up in front of the house, but didn't cut off the bike.

"You not comin' up to give me some of this?" she quipped, sucking on his earlobe and giving his dick a squeeze.

"Next time, mama. I gotta take care of somethin'."

She sucked her teeth and reluctantly got off the bike, standing at full height. In her heels she towered over Swags 5-foot 9-inch stature.

"How many chicks you fuck wit' you can trust?" he questioned.

"None," she retorted.

He chuckled.

"How many you got, you can leash?"

"How many you need, daddy?"

"At least five."

"Then I got you," she assured him, draping her arms around his neck and tonguing him lustfully. His tongue tasted so sweet in her mouth. After the kiss, she added, "And I'ma keep you too."

Swag winked at her, ran his hand over her ass, and told her, "Walk nasty for me."

Just watching her strut inside, he knew he had a thoroughbred.

\* \* \* \* \* \*

Despite the steady drizzle, Antman's funeral was massive. If the worth of a gangsta was in the size of the funeral procession, then Ant was a giant. He was a ladies' man with a wife, three baby mamas, and a rack of jump offs. But they all played their position, so the funeral was drama free. Hustlers, far and wide, came to pay their respects.

As the crowd thinned out, Thump and Love stayed graveside, both holding umbrellas.

Black suits and black derbies cocked ace-deuce.

"Even God cryin' for my nigguh," Thump remarked, tilting his head back and lowering the umbrella to feel the rain on his face. The drops ran down his cheeks like tears.

"Yeah, no doubt," Love agreed.

All three of them had come up together. For a few seconds they were both caught up in their own moment of silence. After a while, Love cleared his throat. He looked around at the retreating crowd and the shooters spread out for security, just in case.

"So what's good?" Love asked.

Thump's face balled up in a look of disgust.

"Fucking nothin', yo. Either nigguhs don't know or real good at sayin' nothing. Ain't no new traps set up, no new crews on the set."

"Then maybe it ain't a crew," Love surmised, referring to the fact it could be one dude.

"Ain't no fuckin' way one muhfucka gonna come at us like that, yo. I'm *tellin'* you it's a sour nigguh in the circle," Thump argued.

Love nodded, looked at the pretty, long-stemmed roses on Ant's gold railed coffin and answered, "Maybe . . . If so, this what you do. Every nigguh from Jo-Jo's crew that was out that night with 'em . . ." Love let his voice trail off. The implications were clear.

Thump nodded.

"I got you."

"And make it ugly. Let's see who flinches," Love added as his phone rang.

He looked at it, smirked, and then put it back without answering.

"A bitch?" Thump surmised.

"Yeah, yo. Lil' slick country bitch I ran into," he replied, using his own inside joke. "She on my dick already."

Thump chuckled.

"Yo, Ant. You hear this pretty boy ass nigguh? Between the two of y'all, I don't know who worse!"

Love laughed because Thump was always the fat, ugly dude. Deep down, Thump felt a way about it. That was a part of the reason he went so hard to make his name with his hands.

Love checked his watch.

"What up? You ready?"

"Naw, I'ma chill a little longer," Thump replied.

Love clapped him on the shoulder.

"That's my word, fam'. We gonna get these nigguhs . . . whoever did it," Love vowed.

"No doubt."

They gave each other a gangsta hug and then Love made his way through the wet grass, hating how stray blades stuck to his gators.

# Chapter Seven

H all handed Jazmine a manila envelope as he rounded the bench and took a seat beside her. The sounds of little kids whooping and ripping around filled the air. They were meeting in a small out of the way park on the outskirts of the city. As long as she was undercover, Hall was careful to keep Jazmine away from the precinct.

She slid the pictures out. They were three different angles of the same gruesome scene, four young thugs beaten with baseball bats beyond recognition. Blood was everywhere. Their faces twisted into expressions of agony, evidence they had died in extreme pain.

She whistled. "This looks personal."

"Very. That is what's left of that kid Jo-Jo's crew. Looks like Love wanted to send a message to whom it may concern," Hall reasoned.

"So I guess he thinks it's an inside job. You and Love think alike," she teased.

"Don't remind me," he retorted.

"Still." She began looking at the pictures again with a morbid curiosity. "This could be playing right into the other crew's hands because Love's eating his own."

"*If* there's another crew," he reminded her.

"Five bucks says you're both wrong."

"You're on. So where are you on this thing?"

"I've got my first date with him tomorrow. I plan on wining, dining . . . and dropping him like a bad habit." She smirked, looking at the children playing and remembering why she hated kids.

Hall glanced at her.

"So what's the punch line? How does that help?"

"He's a pretty boy . . . real pretty. He's never been dropped, so his ego is fragile. Isn't it the Bible that says 'A house divided can't stand?'" she quipped.

"Ah, I think that's the Jewish Bible." he cracked. She got it and laughed. He added, "So what're you doing tonight? You know the game's coming on?"

She flashed a dimpled smile at him sweetly.

"I'm . . . kind of tired, you know? Next time for sure."

Hall smiled knowingly and brushed her long hair off her face, so he could study her profile. "You're one coldhearted bitch, and I mean that as a compliment. Because sometimes you have to be in this man's world. Just . . . try to remember how this game is played, huh? And by the way, I love the new look with the long hair."

They looked at each other. The moment was clear. She had gotten what she wanted, only Hall wanted more. He yearned for her young supple body. She was like the sweetest addiction or the deadliest disease.

"I'll call you," she replied with a hint of promise in her tone, and then walked off.

"Yeah, you do that," he mumbled, watching her walk off.

\* \* \* \* \* \*

"It looks good . . . what is it?" Jazmine quipped, looking at the small grilled piece of meat on her plate, decorated with greenery!

They were at a fancy restaurant named The Metropolitan, a cozy little spot that Love took many of his dates before he fucked them.

He smiled at her ignorance.

"You ain't hear when I ordered it?"

"I heard you say something about some chorzo," she answered.

"Naw ma, *chorizo*. It's grilled sausage with peppers and onions."

She cut a small piece and took a nibble. Her brows rose.

"Okay," she said in an impressed tone. "I like this *chorizo*. It just ain't enough of it."

He chuckled.

"That's the key to life. Always leave 'em wanting more," Love remarked.

"Naw, bro, trust me. That ain't always a good thing," Jazmine corrected him.

He raised his wine glass in a subtle toast.

"I stand corrected."

She took another bite of her sausage.

"So, this where you take all the girls you tryin' to fuck?" she asked with a knowing smirk.

She had put him on the spot with her straight forwardness, but he was too much of a player to let it show.

"Naw, just the ones I want to get to know afterwards."

"Confidence always gets an A plus in my book," she complimented, smiling at him over the rim of her glass.

The dinner went smoothly, both feeding the others' ego and being fed over their dessert of an Italian ice cream called gelato. Jazmine remarked, "I feel like dancing. You?"

His mind said no, because he was ready to get a room, but he replied," Sure, why not."

"You know any good clubs?" she probed, already knowing the answer.

"Yeah, I do," he replied, waving the waiter over for the check. "Mine."

* * * * * *

Love's club, appropriately named Love's was indeed the hottest club in town. It was a converted warehouse that sported three levels and a pool and patio in the back where he threw lock up pool parties that were totally unforgettable.

The line wrapped the block as Love cruised through, and then turned into an alley that led to his private parking area for him and his crew. When he parked he saw Thump's Cadillac XTS and another member of the crew's Porsche Boxster. While his attention was taken by the act of parking, she quickly slipped the small magnetic bugging device under her seat.

Love opened the car door for her, taking her hand like a gentleman and helping her out of the car.

"Who says city boys don't know how to treat a lady?" she joked with a flirtatious tone.

"You ain't seen nothing yet," he shot back, licking his lips as if his last thought was delicious.

He watched her walk up the fire escape, the sway in her hips hypnotic, and the jiggle under her silk dress letting Love know she wasn't wearing any panties. He couldn't wait until the club closed.

The fire escape door opened up into Love's office which doubled as the VIP of the VIP lounge, which took up half of the second floor. The office was walled-in glass, so Love and his crew could see the whole club. In one corner was the pool table where Thump and another dude were playing. A few other major ballers in Love's inner circle lounged around profiling and conversing with the VIP chicks, one of those chicks, a dark-skinned five-star that glowed like the moon dipped in chocolate.

"Hey Love. How you, daddy?" Rain greeted, giving him a hug.

"How you, Rain?" he replied.

Rain looked at Jazmine, frowned like something was wrong, and looked her up and down. Then she turned back to Love.

"Anyway, holla at me, Love. I'm tryin' to talk to you about somethin'," Rain told him as she stepped off with that nasty strut of hers.

Love turned to Jazmine.

"Yo, don't worry about that. That's nobody."

"Do I look like I need to be worried?" she quipped with a smirk.

"Confidence gets an A plus in my book," Love replied, using her line from earlier. Then he added, "Come on. I wanna introduce you to my peoples." They approached the table where Thump and the other dude were playing.

"Yo, Jaz. This my man Lo and my man Thump. This Jazmine," Love said.

Jazmine and Lo exchanged hellos, but it was Thump that she turned her attention to, grabbing eye contact and daring him to look away.

"Thump, huh? Why they call you that?" she asked with naked flirtation, so naked Thump had to look at Love because he was getting his signals crossed.

"Just a hood name, ma. Shit just stuck," Thump answered modestly.

"I'm Jazmine."

"He just told me that."

"Now I'm telling you," she shot back, still maintaining an eye contact his gaze kept darting away and coming back to.

At first, Love was subtly stuck. There had been times when females with Thump had pushed up on him, but never the other way around. He was the Boss. He was the pretty boy, so it was far from the course. But this was something his ego had never experienced, just as Jazmine had anticipated.

"Yeah, yo. Must be a echo in here or something, huh?" he joked weakly, maintaining his player façade.

"Umm, Love?" Jazmine said in her sweetest please voice. "I'm kinda dry. Could you . . ." She let her voice trail off on the request.

For a split second, he got vexed, feeling like she was trying to play him and on some waiter shit, but his ego assured him that surely *no* bitch would play *him* like that.

Jazmine watched the look flitter across his face and read his mind. Just like that, it was gone and he smiled like, "No doubt, ma. What you drinkin'?"

"Grey Goose and cranberry, if it's not too much to ask."

"I got you."

When Love walked away, Jazmine turned back to Thump.

"So, Thump . . . You know how to use this?" She flirted, grabbing his pool cue, sliding her hands up and down it slowly in a suggestive manner before taking it out of his giant hands.

"I do ai'ight," Thump remarked, warming to the conversation.

"Baby, humility is overrated. *Trust,*" she remarked as she bent over the table, set her shot and then released it, combining the nine into the three, dropping it in the side pocket. She handed him back the cue.

"You look like you know somethin' there," Thump remarked, impressed.

# SWAG

"How much you willin' to put up to find out?" she asked, one eyebrow deliciously raised.

"You wanna gamble?" Thump chuckled incredulously, just as Love walked up and handed Jazmine her drink. "Yo, Love. Man, you betta tell your girl somethin' about me and this table here."

Love knew what Thump was really asking. He wanted to know if Jazmine was with him or just came with him. Reluctantly, but nonchalantly, he shrugged like, "Shit, if she wanna play the game . . ."

"Then that's what it is then. Yo, Love, give her that stick, fam'. Lemme school lil' mama right quick," Thump said.

As the game wore on, Love had moved on to schmoozing the room. He talked to Rain, and he talked to two dudes that wanted to do business. Love listened to everybody with only half an ear and one eye because he frequently turned his attention to Thump and Jazmine. His head was totally twisted. That's what mind games do to you.

Jazmine pretended not to notice, but she kept track of him out of the corner of her eyes. She could see her game was working because she knew nothing was more fragile than a man's ego. So she proceeded to crack Love like an egg, scramble it, and then serve it to him in the end.

He drove her home in virtual silence. Despite the occasional small talk and the sounds of his Trey Songz CD, there was no conversation until they got to Jazmine's apartment.

"Are you upset with me?" she asked innocently.

He didn't even bother to cut off the car.

"Upset." He chuckled, masking the vexation. "For what?"

"I'm just sayin'. Like, I had a good time with you at dinner, but it's just . . . Thump . . ." Her voice trailed off like she was at a loss for words.

"Ma, come on. It ain't that serious, trust me," he replied cockily.

"So it wouldn't be an issue if I holla at your man?"

"Naw, shit. We just keep it in the family," he quipped with a subtle hint of disrespect in his tone.

Jazmine smiled to herself, because she knew she had him after that immature comment.

"Do I still get the job?" She snickered.

"Ma, I ain't no petty nigguh. I said I got you, I got you," Love assured her.

She leaned over and kissed him on the cheek. She played him in a sensual way.

"You the man, daddy," she cooed with a hint of mockery in her tone that he missed.

She opened the door, and then looked back over her shoulder.

"You not gonna walk me to my door?"

He laid his head back against the headrest.

"Ma, I'm tired as fuck, yo, but I'ma wait until you get in."

"Yep," she remarked as she got out. *Men are so fuckin' easy to play . . .*

# Chapter Eight

T wenty minutes later, Love met Thump at a closed gas station. They pulled up, driver's door to driver's door.

"What's up, fam'? What's going on?" Thump inquired.

"I wanted to holla at you about that bitch Candy Rain," Love told him.

"The stripper bitch?"

"Yeah."

"Fuck that skan-less bitch talkin' about?"

"She had a nigguh come through the club askin' questions about us. She said he ain't from around here, and he was trying to pick her brain."

"Police?" Thump threw out.

"Or that bitch ass nigguh," Love spat.

Thump thought about it and then replied, "Man, I don't know. I don't trust that black bitch, yo. Why a complete stranger gonna just expose his hand like that?"

"I feel you. But either way, we need to keep our eye on the club 'til we see what's up," Love proposed.

"Indeed."

Thump's phone rang. He checked it, scowled. He didn't recognize the number, so he didn't answer.

"But yo, I'll put somebody on it. Have 'em sit on the club er' night 'til this nigguh show up," Thump told him. Then a text came through. He checked it and a smirk crossed his face. He texted back.

Something told Love it was Jazmine he was texting.

"Yeah, yo. Do that."

"It's done. I'm out."

"Holla."

\* \* \* \* \* \*

Jazmine: *I want some dick*

That was the text Thump got from Jazmine that made him smirk.

Thump: *I deliver.*

She texted him her address. Thump was feeling Jazmine. She was cool, funny, fine, sexy as fuck, and if her text was any indication, a certified freak. It wasn't that Thump wasn't used to bad bitches, but he knew they were usually only after his paper. But he had already convinced himself that wasn't the case with Jazmine. She had chose him over the boss, so if it was about money, he knew most females shot for the top, and he certainly didn't see himself as an easier target than the next man.

Men never do.

He pulled up at Jazmine's complex, got out, and approached the door. He rang the bell once. Jazmine answered the door with her heels, T-shirt, and no panties, which became obvious when she walked away from the door and the bottom of her succulent cheeks played hide and seek with the length of the T-shirt.

"I would offer you a drink, but I ain't got time for all that," Jazmine cooed, leading him to the bedroom.

The way that ass was jiggling made Thump grab his dick and reply, "Shit, I wasn't thirsty anyway."

She glanced over her shoulder and giggled like a naughty schoolgirl.

When they got to the bedroom, Jazmine kicked off the heels and then reached up to wrap herself around Thump's 6-foot 2-inch stature and kissed him with an intensity that made his dick jump.

"Relax, baby, and let me show you what's been on my mind since I met you," she whispered, guiding him to sit on the bed.

Jazmine unbuttoned his shirt, kissing along his chest and flicking her tongue over his nipples and along his ample stomach. She unbuttoned his jeans, pulling them down to his ankles. His thick but short dick stood rigid and veiny as she wrapped her lips around it and began bobbing on it slowly.

Thump's toes curled in his gator boots.

Jazmine was doing her best Pinkie impression, slurping and moaning in order to add to the intensity of the moment. She began sucking with no hands, keeping the rhythm, but picking up the pace. She could feel the rumble building in him, so with a final wet slurp, mouth and cheeks wet, she took his dick out her mouth.

"Uh-un, not until I get mine." She smirked.

She pushed him back on the bed and climbed on top of him, grabbed his dick and slid it inside her wet pussy. His girth pushed her walls to its limits, filling her up and making her fuck him harder.

"Oh my God!" she gushed, "It's soooo thick!"

Thump was trying his damnedest not to bust so soon, but Jazmine's pussy was so wet, soft and tight, he felt like he was fucking a virgin with experience. Jazmine worked her hips and inner muscle, holding nothing back, because first impressions left lasting impressions.

Thump couldn't hold it anymore and skeeted inside her, falling short of three minutes. She used her muscles to squeeze out every drop, making Thump shiver.

"Gotdamn, lil' mama! You don't put no cut on it, do you?" Thump chuckled, feeling embarrassed. "A nigguh could usually fuck all night. You got me bustin' like a young boy."

She knew his ego was vulnerable, so she slid under him with game strong enough to prop it back up. Jazmine lay her head on his chest and replied, "Don't worry, we got all the time in the world to fuck all night. Lessen' you don't wanna one night stand?"

"Naw, ma, definitely not," Thump admitted.

Jazmine looked up into his eyes and said, "Baby, ain't no use in me lyin'. I'm feeling you. Layin' here, cuddled up on your chest, got me feeling like a lil' ol' bitty girl, and I ain't never felt like that befo'. I ain't stupid, though. I know you got bitches left and right, so I know you gonna do you. But just make sure you come through and do me." Jazmine winked seductively, her drawl, molasses thick and just as artificially sweet.

Southern girls made the best cons and the strongest men, the easiest conned. Thump never saw it coming. All he saw was a doe-eyed country girl that needed a man like him in her life.

He caressed her cheek and replied, "Just play your cards right, ma, and we'll be doin' us."

Jazmine smiled, and then slid over his belly and bowed to her Budha.

*  *  *  *  *  *

"Fuck that skan-less bitch talkin' about."

Thump's voice filled Hall's office. Jazmine was playing back the conversation she had recorded with the bugging device planted in Love's car. It was a powerful device that transmitted sound through the air in microwaves, and cut itself on and off through the detection of human voices.

Hall stopped the recording. It was the second time he had played it.

"So who the hell is Candy Rain?" Hall asked.

"A stripper," Jazmine quipped, referring to Thump's comment on the tape.

"Smart ass," Hall growled. "I mean, besides a stripper. What role does she play in the crew?"

"I don't think she plays any role," Jazmine surmised. "She was just there to talk to Love. Apparently, to tell him this. I guess she was trying to score brownie points," Jazmine concluded, remembering the look Rain had given her. The irony made her chuckle.

"What is so funny?"

"Nothing."

Hall gave her a curious look, but let it go. He leaned over his computer and typed. "C-A-N- . . . think she spells it D-Y or D-I?"

"Try both."

"D . . . Y . . . RAIN. Bingo! Shawnette Haynes, 23. She has a couple of priors for assaults."

"Tough girl," Jazmine remarked.

"Tell me about it . . . okay, so now it's starting to look like you were right. It may be an outside crew."

Jazmine playfully popped her collar.

"Beginner's luck." He chuckled.

"This was a lucky break, too. Because now we know that Love's gonna have a few guys at that club waitin' on this guy. Now if we sit on them, and maybe catch a couple of lackeys for murder one, I'll betcha another five dollars that'll give us a chance to get 'em to turn on Love," she proposed.

Hall raised an eyebrow.

"Murder one? Don't you mean *attempted* murder?" Hall probed.

Jazmine smiled coldly.

"Detective, we didn't have a warrant for that bug, so legally, we don't know a murder's being planned, now do we? And if they kill this guy, we really can't stop 'em, now can we?"

Hall shook his head admiringly.

"Cold-blooded . . ." he complimented her, because deep down he agreed. If it meant some thug got killed so they could get Love, so be it.

Jazmine stood up to leave.

"So I presume you'll take the appropriate measures?"

"I'm way ahead of you." Jazmine held out her hand.

"What?"

"Umm, that five you owe me. If you don't mind?" she snickered.

He went in his pocket, peeled a five, and put it in her hand. But when she tried to pocket it, he held on.

"But ahh, I think it's time you pay up, too, huh?"

The look in his eyes was subtle, but she saw the danger involved in playing with people's emotions.

"How does eight sound?"

Hall didn't answer. He just let the bill go and she walked out.

# Chapter Nine

F or three nights in a row, Swag merged with the shadows across the street from the club. He didn't see the unmarked police until the second night, but by the third night, he was ready to make his move. He watched as Rain got in a car with two dudes and smiled to himself, thinking about the conversation that led up to this.

*"Daddy, you buggin'! Love? Like, you ain't from around here, so let me tell you. Love—is no joke,"* Rain had warned him.

*"Neither am I,"* Swag shot back. *"Just do what the fuck I ask you, ai'ight? You wit' me or him?"*

*"You, but—"*

*"No buts, ma-ma. We rock 100 or we don't rock at all. Just go to the club tonight and holla at 'im! Tell 'im I'm new in town, and I was tryna' pick your brain about him. Then fall back. You ain't involved, yo. I got you,"* Swag assured her, using the same line he used on Michelle.

*"Okay, daddy,"* Rain agreed reluctantly.

"I got you." Swag smirked as he watched the car pull off. He checked the police one more time, and then cranked up his bike and followed the dark green Chevy, but never turned his headlight on.

Swag followed them to Rain's house. The guys dropped her off and then they left. He tailed them to a McDonald's with an all night drive thru. The Chevy was the only car in line.

"Yo, man, I'm fuckin' tired of that shit, yo. Waitin' for this nigguh 'er night!" the driver griped after placing their order.

"Yeah, well, tell Love that," the passenger shot back. "He want this nigguh bad."

"So how the fuck long we 'posed to do this?"

"As long as it take."

"Or until he gets you."

It took them both a blink of a second to realize the comment didn't come from the other. Swag had snuck up alongside the passenger side. By the time they realized this, it was too late.

"Fuck!" the passenger gruffed, trying to pull out his gun.

Swag was toying with them, to the point where the driver almost had his gun raised, but Swag aimed and started dumping shot after shot into the car through the open passenger window, blowing the passenger's brain all over the driver and the driver's brain all over the screaming girl in the drive thru window. Had she not had the presence of mind to duck and get away from the window, Swag would've killed her too, because he believed in no witnesses.

He tucked the gun and ran back to the dumpster where he had left his bike still running. He jumped on, gunned the bike so hard it wheeled, and then he disappeared into the night.

Swag shot back to Rain's house. He parked his bike on the street behind Rain's street and took the backyards to her house. Cautiously, he climbed the back stairs to the back door, listened intently for a moment, and then knocked lightly. Swag didn't hear any movement. He peered through the window. The house was completely dark, but he could see straight through to the front door, the silhouette of a staircase on the right side of the hallway.

He knocked again, this time, pulling out his gun and clicking off the safety. He heard steps and saw Rain approaching the door cautiously.

She peered out and then frowned a little with a puzzled expression.

"Swag?"

"Open the door."

She did. As soon as he was in, he headed for the front of the house.

"Why you come to the back—"

He cut her off. "Yo, get your stuff. We gotta go," he instructed her, looking in both front rooms. Satisfied that no one was there, he turned his full attention to her, but still didn't put up the gun.

She looked at it, uneasy.

"Why?" Rain probed.

"'Cause you ain't safe here," he replied, matter of factly.

"Why wouldn't I be—" she started to say and then it hit her. She remembered the ride home. Once, when the car turned a corner, out of the corner of her eye, she thought she saw an all black motorcycle with no headlights, but she wasn't sure. But by the second corner, she was. Now she knew why.

"Swag, you killed them, didn't you?"

He glared at her.

"Just get your shit. Or you want Love comin' here askin' why his peoples is leakin'?"

Rain shook her head.

"You did it on purpose. You did it to lock me in," she surmised, and his non-response told her she was right. "What? You ain't trust me?"

"I don't trust nobody, but I know everybody can trust themselves to survive," he replied, stone faced.

Swag knew by killing the two shooters, Love would think Rain help set them up. Now, she couldn't cross Swag even if she wanted to, because he was now her lifeline.

"Daddy, you ain't have to do me like that. I was wit' you from the door," she told him.

"You still wit' me?"

"Yes! But I'm still gonna whoop your ass," she quipped.

Swag smiled.

"Just go get your stuff."

"Mama, who that?"

Neither of them had noticed that Rain's three-year-old daughter Renee had come downstairs rubbing her eyes.

"That's your new daddy, Swag." Rain giggled.

"That ain't my daddy!" Renee protested as Swag picked her up. She looked at him and said, "You look funny."

Swag chuckled. He handed her to Rain.

"You know I'm taking her, right?" Rain said.

He shrugged.

"Whateva'. What up wit' those three girls I told you to get at?"

"Ain't none of em' cut for this, but I know somebody who is?"

"Who?"

"My cousin, Gotti," Rain answered.

Swag thought about it a moment, and then asked, "Where he at?"

"Upstairs."

"Take me to holla at him."

Gotti was Rain's young, wild cousin. He was only twenty-two and had already done six years in and out of jail, juvenile detention, and prison. He was a hard head with a serious hammer game that was like he had nothing to lose.

When Rain and Swag walked in, Gotti was sitting on the bed watching an episode of *The Wire*. A close-up of Omar's fierce scowl filled the screen. Swag looked at Gotti and knew he was a beast. He had his shirt off, revealing a chiseled frame bulging from prison iron. A scar ran down his neck from behind his ear, a prison moment from juvy. He had dark skin like Rain with a sleepy-eyed sneer that reminded a lot of people of a young Big Daddy Kane.

When Gotti saw Swag, he stared him down hard with a glint of recognition in his gaze, a look Swag returned with equal intensity. Far from a look of aggression, it was like they both instantly grasped the cut of the other at first glance.

"Yo, Rain, who dis?" Gotti gruffed.

"Swag, yo," Swag answered, stepping forward and offering his hand.

Gotti took it.

"Yo, what's good?" Gotti inquired.

"Rain says you just came home. What up? You tryin' to get money?"

"Fuck yeah. What you got in mind?"

"Love."

"Love?"

Gotti frowned at Rain like, "Yo, is the nigguh sane?" Then his scowl turned into a menacing grin. *Yeah, I definitely like you, nigguh!*

He stood up, towering over Swag like the Hulk, punching his hand with his fist.

"Ay yo, I been waitin' for a muthafucka wit' heart to take it to that pussy! His whole team bitch, yo. The only one jive real is Thump! But fuck him too. Them nigguhs been eatin' too long. Real talk! I'm wit' it, yo. Put me down wit' the team!"

Swag smiled mischievously.

"Ain't no team . . . It's me . . . now you."

Gotti looked at Rain again.

"Yeah, this nigguh got a death wish . . . but that's the only way to win. He don't give a fuck about losin'!" Gotti barked and then laughed.

His cackle sounded so crazy, Rain and Swag laughed too.

"You two must've been made for one another," Rain cracked, shaking her head.

She didn't know how right she was . . .

"So, what's the plan?" Gotti questioned.

"We win, they lose. Whatever it takes!" Swag replied. "All I got is enough guns and a steady connect."

"Guns and butter, baby." Gotti smirked, giving Swag dap. "Let's get it."

# Chapter Ten

Y es, Allan. The shooting in the wee hours of the morning at this McDonald's that you see here behind me," the female reporter said, gesturing to the McDonald's drive thru, which was surrounded with yellow crime scene tape. "Two men, both in their early twenties, were brutally gunned down as they waited in the drive-thru. One witness, who wishes to remain anonymous, said he came out of nowhere. "All I could do is duck and pray."

Thump turned his attention to Love.

"Now you see why I don't trust that bitch!" he growled.

Love was seething. His jaw line went rigid as he flexed his jaw muscles. They were in the back of Love's urban clothing store. He turned off the TV and stood up, his mind burning with the image of Rain's face.

"Find that bitch, yo. I don't give a fuck if you gotta drag her off the goddamn pole! Feel me!"

Love felt like Rain had played him to his face, and for that, there was no forgiveness. Just like Swag had planned. He wanted to make sure all Rain's bridges were burnt.

Thump nodded.

"Ay, yo. I say we call this nigguh . . . see if he still got Ant phone. Rock 'im to sleep, bring 'im out in the open, and make sure we don't miss," Thump proposed.

Love bit his bottom lip pensively.

"Not yet . . . real talk, this nigguh ain't no dummy. The way he move . . . nah. Right now we in the blind. He ain't. He know somethin' we don't. Nah, we don't do nothin'! Let him think we shook. He'll overplay his hand sooner or later."

"Yo, fuck that sooner or later shit, Love! He ain't gotta *think* we shook. We *look* shook! These nigguhs out here keepin' score. Every time we don't holla back, niggas get *bolder*. Wanna try they hand. Somebody know somethin'! If it ain't Rain, it's her mother. Her goddamn grandmama. I don't give a fuck! I'ma get at this nigguh," Thump ranted.

Even though Love never liked for someone to question his authority, he knew why his man was upset.

"Fam', I feel you, and you *know* I loved Ant, too. But this is bigger than Ant, yo. We *gonna* get this nigguh, that's no question. But if we set the city ablaze, that heat gonna be on *us*, feel me? Stay on the same page," Love concluded.

Thump just looked at Love. Love had always been the thinker in the crew, something Thump both envied and admired. But it was times like these that really brought out the difference in their approaches.

"Yeah, ai'ight," Thump reluctantly agreed.

They heard a light knock at the door.

"Yo," Love called out.

One of the beautiful chicks Love had working at the store peeked in.

"Umm, Thump. It's some chick out here lookin' for you. What you want me to tell her?"

"Tell her I'm on my way out," he replied.

The chick closed the door.

"Yo, you and shorty might as well get joined at the hip." Love chuckled, feeling no malice but not forgetting either.

Thump smiled.

"Naw, yo, it ain't like that. Shorty good peoples, that's all," he answered, heading for the door.

"Let me find out you fallin' in love."

Thump paused at the door. "Fuck that. But still you know what they say, Every Thug Needs A Lady."

"Yeah, but it was a chick that said it!" Love laughed and made Thump laugh too.

When Thump came out, Jazmine was at the counter buying a man's sweater.

"Ma, what you doin'?" Thump frowned.

"I just got my first check today, and I saw this sweater, so I wanted to see you in it," Jazmine answered.

It was a simple gesture, but it made Thump smile. A chick had never bought him anything; they just wanted to be bought.

"Naw, man," he protested, turning to the cashier. "Yo, give her back her money."

The cashier did.

"We royalty around here. Matter of fact, Tina, gimme that Red Atlanta snapback, too."

She handed it to him. He put it on Jazmine, cocked ace-deuce.

"Somethin' for you, somethin' for me," he quipped, putting the sweater over his shoulder as they walked out.

Jazmine had been working at Love's non-profit for a week, but the last couple of days she had been driving Thump's Caddy to work, because her car was in the shop. As they approached the car, she asked, "You want me to drive? You look tired."

"Naw, ma, I'm good. Just got shit on my mind."

She tossed him the keys and they got in.

"Like what?" she probed.

"Just shit, yo," he responded as he started up the car.

"Business, huh?" she asked.

He chuckled.

"Yeah . . . business."

"Maybe I can help. 'Cause you know in Georgia, we beez in the trap, beez-beez in the trap," she sang in a silly tone, making him laugh.

"You crazy, yo," Thump remarked.

"I just hate to see you stressed." Jazmine pouted, rubbing the back of his neck.

Thump shrugged like, "Part of the job description."

"Well, if you can't talk to me, I might as well be on *my* job description," she replied mischievously.

Jazmine turned her hat to the back and leaned over and began to undo his jeans.

"Yo, Jaz, I'm drivin' here. What you doin'?"

"My job," she answered, pulling his sausage-like dick out and began to tongue kiss it awake.

Thump was getting used to this kind of treatment, because for the past three days after work, she fed him, fucked and sucked him until it was time for him to hit the streets every night. She was definitely playing her position, her every position, any position he desired.

The heavenly sensation in his lap made him swerve like he was drunk.

"Gotdamn, ma! You gonna make me wreck this muthafucka."

She looked at him, eyes equally innocent and lustful.

"You want me to stop?"

"Fuck no!" he answered, pushing her head back down into his lap.

He got to a red light and thanked God for it. Her head was bobbing wildly enough for the driver in the next lane to just look over and see a porno flick. But Thump was oblivious to the voyeur. His head was back, eyes closed, totally slipping in the middle of the street. The light turned green. The Caddy didn't budge. Cars behind him blew their horn. He didn't care. By now he had one hand on the back of Jazmine's head and his other hand has found its way into the back of her jeans, finger-fucking her in the ass, something that drove her crazy. She sucked harder as he fucked her face. Cars went around him just as he was about to bust. He heard the familiar whoop of the police siren. His eyes popped open and his body spasmed at the same time. He looked to his right and looked into the face of a stone-faced cop. He couldn't do anything but sink into the comfort of the release of the momentous load he just shot down Jazmine's throat. Thump was expecting to get pulled over, however, the officer just grinned, gave him the thumbs up, and pulled off.

\* \* \* \* \* \*

They laughed about it, all the way to her complex.

"Yo, you shoulda saw the look on your face," Jazmine teased.

"You shoulda seen what was in yours," he shot back, playfully grabbing her ass and pulling her to him by her back pocket.

Jazmine slapped his hand away.

"Stop. We got all night for that, because *tonight*, you chillin' wit' me," she demanded.

"I—" he began, but she cut him off.

She smirked.

"I, nothin'. We chillin' tonight. Now what you want to eat?"

"I don't know. Where you wanna go?"

"No, I mean *eat*, eat. I feel like cookin', so you better take advantage while you can," she told him as she headed into the kitchen.

"I know that's right."

Thump leaned against the doorway to the kitchen and watched her move around, taking out pans and washing her hands. His eyes travelled along the curves of her body, and over the profile of her face as he thought how much of a total package she was. Smart, sexy, funny and definitely a freak. All those qualities added up to wifey material. He would test her, make her jump through hoops and walk through fire, but the whole while, he'd be praying she passed the test, because deep down, he wanted her to be The One.

Jazmine saw Thump admiring her from the doorway and took a deep breath in her mind. Her game was on 1,000 and she knew it, but the move she was about to make would make or break the whole plan. If she missed, it was over, but either way, there was no turning back now.

"Well, if you ain't gonna answer, I'ma fry some chicken and make some fries," she decided.

"That's cool."

She got the chicken quarters out of the refrigerator. As she laid them on the counter, she looked over at him. "What? Why you looking at me like that?"

Thump shrugged. "Just thinkin', ma"

"About?"

"Life."

Jazmine smiled knowingly.

"Baby, I know you ain't used to talkin', but believe me. You can trust me. I'm wit' you."

"Trust is a big word wit' me, ma. It ain't somethin' I take lightly," he replied.

"Neither do I," she affirmed, looking him in his eyes. "I been through too much in my life to play games, Deon," she added, calling him by his real name.

"Yeah, me too."

They looked at one another briefly, two people weary of relationships, both with their own hang-ups, but only one sincerely wanting to get past them.

"So, when I say I'm wit' you, I'm wit' you," Jazmine remarked, adding, "just like wit' your business. I can help you with that."

Thump chuckled. "Yeah? What makes you so sure?"

Jazmine wiped her hands on the dish towel, stepped closer to him, looked him in the eyes and said, "'Cause I'm a cop."

At first, Thump chuckled, thinking she was playing. But when he looked at her again and saw that her expression still hadn't changed, he shook his head.

"What!" he growled, his temperature rising with every breath.

Jazmine sensed it and tried to speak.

"Baby, I—" That's all she got out, before Thump backhanded the shit out of her and sent her half way across the kitchen.

He had dazed her, but her adrenaline was flowing and her reflexes were quick. As she got up, she snatched the small .25 caliber from her ankle holster.

Seeing her pull a gun, he reached to the small of his back and came out with his .45. Both aimed for the other's head.

"Baby, *listen* to *me*! *Listen*!"

"Shut the fuck up!" he barked.

His anger burned with a sense of betrayal. Like somebody had been playing his favorite song and then snatched the needle across it, bringing it to an abrupt end. Cop? He couldn't wrap his mind around what was going on.

"NO! I won't shut up. *Listen*! . . . Okay, look," Jazmine began as she lowered her gun, and then let it drop to the floor. She raised her hands.

"You gonna shoot me? Shoot."

Thump gripped the gun as if that was exactly what he intended to do. She knew he wouldn't, and it wasn't because she was a cop.

"Baby," she said softly, taking the syrup out of her drawl, but not the twang. "I didn't have to tell you that . . . I didn't. They sent me undercover to take you and Love down . . . that was my assignment. Think about that. *Think* . . . I didn't have to tell you."

Jazmine could see the war in his eyes. His brain and heart wanted to believe, but his gut was telling him no. She stepped cautiously forward.

"I told you if I'm wit' you, I'm wit' you. Look at me. Nothing has changed. I'm on your side. I'm wit' you. If I wanted to take you down I wouldn't have exposed myself. I told you because I trust you, baby. Now I need you to trust me."

By the time she completed her lullaby, she was right in front of him, the barrel inches from her face. She did it purposely to give Thump the visual of the gun in her face. She knew that would make him lower the gun. Slowly, reluctantly, he did.

"I'm not a cop. The cops just think I'm one," she remarked, a hint of a devilish grin playing across her face.

Thump rubbed his forehead.

"Yo, this shit . . . this shit crazy."

In his indecision, Jazmine took charge. She wrapped her arms around his neck and said, "No, it makes *perfect* sense. Now *you* got somebody on the inside. I can find out *anything*. Who's snitchin', who hot, who gonna get raided. We move smart, we can play this shit for all it's worth. Trust me, baby. I'm wit' you," she repeated.

He untangled her arms from around his neck and went in the living room.

"How the fuck I'ma tell Love?"

She followed him.

"Not yet, you can't."

"Why not?" he snapped, looking at her skeptically.

Jazmine took a deep breath.

"Because . . . Love may not be who you think he is."

Thump spazzed. "Bitch, is you crazy! That's my muhfuckin' man. I grew up wit' this nigguh! Fuck you mean he . . ."

"I'm not saying he's *anything*. I just *don't . . . know*," she emphasized expertly, sowing the seed of doubt because she knew accusations worked best when they're not certain.

Thump glared at her.

"Fuck make you say some shit like that?"

"Hall, the chief narcotics detective, thinks the Feds have somebody in the crew. At first he thought it was Ant, but Ant's dead . . . that only leaves you or Love."

Every word was like a strand of the web she was weaving, just like the black widow of deception.

Thump couldn't believe his ears, but one thing he knew about the streets, only those close to you can hurt you. But Love? His man?

"Naw . . . naw, yo. Fuck no!" he growled, protesting to his inner thoughts, out loud.

"Just give me ninety days, and I'll know, okay?" she proposed. "Ninety days, and if I can't say for sure, then I'll tell him myself. In the meantime, let me help you, help *us*. I'm a soldier, baby. Just please . . . trust me," she cooed softly, caressing his face with her fingers, and his ego with a sigh.

Thump eyed her for a moment, like he was looking into the soul she didn't have. He did it so long she got nervous that he would see that nothing was there. Finally, he said, "Ninety days." Then he headed for the door and walked out.

# ANGEL SANTOS

# Chapter Eleven

Y ou did *what!*"
These were the words Hall roared when Jazmine told him she had blown her cover on purpose. They had met on the outskirts of town in the abandoned industrial area, so his words echoed off the towering walls of brick surrounding them. He even dislodged a few birds from their nests. Jazmine however, took it in stride.

"Detective, don't you have high blood pressure or something you need to be watching?" she quipped, trying to make light of the situation.

He pointed at her, and with a curled up lip spat, "Don't get cute. Don't get fuckin' cute when you did something as stupid as this!" He paced in front of her. "That's it! It's over. I'm calling you in."

"Detective, you can't—"

"I *can*, and I just *did*. Are you crazy? Do you have a death wish? You tell two certified killers you're a cop sent undercover to take them to jail and—and—and you expect them to trust you? I would laugh, but I'm too close to tears."

Jazmine anticipated Hall's reaction, or rather, over reaction. But she knew what she was doing, and she believed in her power of persuasion.

"First of all, I didn't tell *both* of them. I only told Thump. Secondly, if it was that serious, I wouldn't be here *now*," she emphasized, looking Hall in the eyes. "Don't you see—"

"I see you're crazy."

"And I see you ain't caught Love yet," Jazmine shot back without missing a beat. The jab stuck him, so she used the opening to make a point. "You want Love. *This* is how we get him. These guys are smart. It'll take years to get them to trust me, and even then, the likelihood of them letting me into the inner circle is next to nil. But this way, it's like Thump is *my* confidential informer, because he *thinks* I'm his dirty cop! It's the same relationship! And with me planting the seed in Thump's head that Love may be a snitch, I can play that rift to the brink. Ninety days, detective, and I'll give you . . . Love," she said, ending her words, articulating the last word with playful tongue action.

Listening to her break down the whole strategy, he truly saw how her mind worked diabolically.

"You were planning this the whole time, huh? This is what you meant when you said you'd beat him with your head?" Hall surmised.

Jazmine smiled.

"Would you have let me go in had I told you from jump?"

"Hell no."

"Then, better to seek forgiveness than seek permission, huh?"

He snorted with amusement and a shake of his head. "Guess we're lucky you're on our side, huh, Georgia?" he signified.

"What other side is there? Ninety days, detective . . . that's all I need."

Hall contemplated it and then asked, "What makes you so sure?"

# S W A G

She opened her car door, looked back over her shoulder with a playful look, and replied, "Because men are so easy to play." Then she blew him a kiss and drove away.

\* \* \* \* \* \*

Thump entered the club with four shooters on his back. The metal detector at the door went crazy, but that didn't even break their stride. Thump looked the bouncer at the door in the eyes as he walked by. The bouncer looked away. He knew better than to object. Besides, he knew Thump hadn't come to be trouble. Or at least he hoped so.

Outside the club, two more carloads of goons sat locked and loaded, eyes peeled. But only no one knew who they were looking for, they just knew to be looking.

Thump didn't know who to look for either, but he knew *what* to look for, eye contact. A challenge. Anybody unlucky enough to be a face out of place that night. On stage, two thick ass red bones lay in a sixty-nine position, giving each other tongue love. Thump didn't even notice. His eyes stayed on scanning the crowd.

The two chicks completed their show and came over to Thump. Their names were Tosha and Mona. They looked like twins, but they weren't even sisters. It was all in the blue contacts and the makeup.

"Hey boo. Long time no see," Mona greeted Thump. She was the thicker of the two and the most scandalous.

"Yo, what up? Where Rain at?" Thump questioned, cutting out the small talk.

By his tone, they knew he was all business.

"She ain't been here in a few days. I don't know. Why? What's up?" Mona wanted to know.

"I'm lookin' for her, that's all, and if you find her it's more where that came from," Thump explained as he handed them both several big faces.

"Shit, say no more," Mona replied.

"Yeah," Thump grunted and walked away.

He hit off a few more strippers the same way. He knew it was only a matter of time before she would be found . . . and then lost.

* * * * * *

Gotti and three of his goons parked the hooptie on 'the block' and got out. Fiends shuffled back and forth looking ashy and sickly in the glare of the sun. In the distance, a car system knocked Ace Hood's "Hustle Hard". The young hustlers on shift ran the block like a well-oiled machine. That is, until Gotti came and threw a monkey wrench in the works.

"Ay, yo. Yo, come 'ere," Gotti called out a female fiend crossing the street. When she just glanced at him and kept going, he added, "Bitch, I know you hear me talkin' to you! What you need? Two for one, come 'ere."

When she heard the double up, she did a one-eighty and shot back over to Gotti. Two young hustlers, one the new block lieutenant in place of Jo-Jo looked on. She completed the transaction, and then the lieutenant and his man stepped to Gotti.

"Ay, yo. Gotti, what the fuck you doin', yo?"

Gotti straightened out the crumbled up bills and didn't even look up.

"Gettin' this gwop, nigguh. Fuck you think?"

"Naw, duke. This Love block, duke. Take that shit somewhere else," the lieutenant warned. His man pulled out a gun and rested it against his thigh. Gotti looked at the lieutenant, and then at the gun.

"Love block? Who the fuck is Love?"

"Who the fuck is *you*?" the gunman hissed.

# SWAG

"Nigguh, what! You gonna shoot me, huh?" Gotti chuckled, looking the gunman dead in the eyes, using that venomous stare he perfected on the prison yard.

Gotti stepped toward him. The gun made the dude feel bold, but the stare had him frozen cold.

Gotti could see the young dude was a bitch at heart, a quality he could quickly assess.

Without a warning, Gotti launched a long armed, overhand right that broke dude's jaw with an audible crack. He was sleep on his feet and only woke up when he hit the ground. Gotti picked up the gun and put it under the lieutenant's chin.

"Get yo' bitch ass against the wall," Gotti hissed, shoving him up against it.

He snatched the other dude off the ground and swung him against it too, and then waved the gun at three other hustlers.

"Y'all too! Get the fuck on the wall, nigguhs. Roll call!"

Because the block had been so hot, none of them were armed except the gunman. But Gotti didn't see one dude on the corner melt into the crowd across the street and run around the corner.

"Roll call! Strip!" he barked with a devilish chuckle.

Jewels clanged and banged as they came off necks and wrists.

"Y'all nigguhs tell Love I wanna see 'im. I need my dick sucked anyway."

Gotti's goons positioned in the street and all armed with revolvers, laughed.

The dude that melted around the corner came back with a gun bigger than him. It was a big body chopper that rocked cars on their axles and chipped bricks when it hit the building. It lifted one of Gotti's goons off his feet, but luckily only hit him in the shoulder, as they scrambled to take cover.

"Gotdamn!" Gotti laughed as he took cover behind the building. "This lil' niggah ain't playin'! Where the fuck he get that gun? Beirut!"

He pulled out his phone and hit send. It was answered instantly.

"Come thru."

"Yep!"

Not even thirty seconds later, a van took the corner, damn near on two wheels. The sliding door flew open, and several barrels of varying calibers came out blazing. The one-man shoot-out ended almost as quickly as it started. Gotti's goons gunned the young boy down. The coroner would find five different types of calibers throughout his body.

By the time Gotti and his team came out, the block looked like a ghost town. The only thing moving was the trash blowing in the street.

"I guess that's why they call it a street sweeper, huh?" Gotti chuckled." I slept on them lil' nigguhs. Let's go."

\* \* \* \* \* \*

Swag woke up from his catnap with Rain's daughter, Renee hitting him on his bulletproof vested chest with a flyswatter.

"Why your chest so hard?" she asked with three-year-old sass.

"'Cause I'm Superman," he croaked in his smoky rasp.

"Na-uh, ain't no such thing as no Superman," Renee shot back.

Swag laughed and sat up when he picked her up. He saw out the corner of his eyes that he wasn't alone. Gotti sat in the corner, looking at him with a penetrating gaze. Swag disregarded it.

"I ain't wanna wake you," Gotti remarked, answering the unasked. "Shit is all good."

"Yeah?"

"Shit gonna be hot, but them nigguhs don't really want it. I been told nigguhs Love and them wasn't cut like that. Now we gonna prove it."

"No doubt," Swag agreed.

An awkward silence ensued.

"Yo, where you from, Swag? New York?"

"Nah, Boston."

"Dorchester?"

"Roxberry."

Gotti nodded. Swag could tell Gotti had something on his mind, but he didn't voice it.

Gotti stood up. He stopped at the door and looked back at Swag.

"Ay, yo. You ever did a bid?"

"Naw."

"That's what I thought," Gotti mumbled as he walked out.

The conversation was more about what wasn't said than what was.

# Chapter Twelve

T hump cracked the bottle of Moet and then poured half of it over Ant's grave. The liquid drenched the grass and began to seep into the ground. He then took a big gulp and looked up at the setting sun.

"Yeah, nigguh. I know you loved that Moet. If it was up to me, it woulda been that Ace." Thump chuckled, and then took another swig. "'Cause this shit go flat too quick . . . Yo, my nigguh. I don't know what the fuck is goin' on. Shit is crazy. Fuckin' Love, yo . . ." Thump said, shaking his head. "I don't understand this nigguh. Them nigguhs came through the block and laid shit down, yo. Now they out there eatin' like shit is sweet, and this nigguh say chill. Fall back. Real talk, I ain't even gonna tell you what shorty said. I can't believe it myself. I don't *wanna* believe it," Thump concluded, took another gulp, and then added, "Shorty's a fuckin' cop, yo . . . I mean, it definitely ain't like *that*. She on my team. I ain't on hers. But still . . . That shit fucked me up at first. But I can't front. I'm type feelin' shorty. She got the wifey qualities, plus she a freak!" He laughed, and then after his laughter subsided, he said, "'Cause I ain't the flyest muhfucka in the world. Shit, you and Love was the pretty boys, but shorty feelin' a nigguh just because, yo . . . it ain't about the money. I done seen gold diggers, and Jaz ain't on it like that. Real talk, dog. If she play her cards right, she could be the one." Thump downed the bottle, not knowing at that very moment, she was playing her cards—her trump card.

Sex.

* * * * * *

It happened when Love came to her office at the mentoring agency. She was sitting at the receptionist desk on the phone when Love walked in with Councilman Joyner. Jazmine was looking scrumptiously professional in her gold frames, long hair up in a bun with one bang flowing along the side of her face, courtesy of Perfect Hair Collection. They walked in just as she hung up the phone.

"Yo, Jaz. I want you to meet somebody. The next mayor of the city," Love said, introducing Joyner.

Joyner chuckled.

"That remains to be seen. For now, just call me Councilman James Joyner," he said as he shook her hand.

"Jazmine Monroe," she answered.

"Ma, hold my calls, ai'ight?" Love requested, as he and Joyner disappeared in his office.

"No problem."

A half hour later, Joyner came out with Love seeing him to the door. Once Joyner was gone, Love turned to Jazmine and said, "Ay, yo. Come in my office for a minute."

She thought nothing of it, because he had called her in his office several times before. When she entered, Love turned to her and said, "Listen, I wanted to introduce him to you because a lot of messages are gonna pass through this office from me to him, but indirectly, feel me?"

"Sort of," she answered, her interest piqued but concealed.

"Nothin' serious. Just . . . duke runnin' for mayor, and he don't want people to jump to conclusions if they see him wit' me."

She nodded. "I got you."

"Matter of fact, he wasn't even here today."

"Who wasn't here today?" She smirked.

Love chuckled. "That's my girl."

"You know I got you."

"I know that's right."

"What?" She giggled as if she didn't know.

Love smiled, like, *You know*. But instead he said, "I like them glasses."

"I been had these."

"You wear 'em for sport, or are you blind?"

"When I need to be," she flirted.

The look she gave Love let him know the next move was on him, which prompted him to remark, "Yo, you like to play games, don't you?"

"Why you say that?"

"Nothin'. Come 'ere. Let me see your glasses," he instructed her.

She crossed the room with that natural strut that drove him crazy every time he saw it. She took off the glasses and handed them to him.

"And if I wanted to play games, I'd say I know you wanna fuck me. Don't you, Love? You wanna beat this pussy. Don't you, Love? If I wanted to play games, I'd make you take it," she purred, sounding like blackberry molasses.

Looking in her eyes, all he could think about was, *This is my man's girl*. He loved Thump like a brother. But deep down, Jazmine had threw him by choosing Thump over him. Shit like that didn't happen to him, so every time she strutted by, he thought about it. Watched that ass jiggle like it was jiggling at him, teasing him, enticing him.

Love tossed her glasses on the desk, and then grabbed her by the back of the neck and pulled her face to his. He devoured her tongue like he had been waiting to do just that, and she fed it to him like the chef she was. Indeed, she had been stewing him for a while on slow simmer, with her sly glances, vocal inflections, and sultry stride. She knew it was only a matter of time.

While snatching her skirt up, Love growled in her ear, "You a nasty bitch, ain't you?"

"Yes," Jazmine whimpered, "treat me like one, daddy."

Love spun her around and bent her flat over his desk. Her pretty brown ass quivered with anticipation, her moist fragrance already making itself felt. Love dropped his pants around his ankles and plowed into her with his long, hard dick making Jazmine cry out of pain. His thrusts drove her to her tippy toes until she caught his rhythm, and then she threw it back to him, thrust for thrust.

"Yeah, daddy. Ohhh, just like that. Fuck this nasty bitch!" she urged him.

Love gripped her bun, pulling it partially loose and began pounding that pussy, trying to make her feel it in her stomach.

"Gotdamn!" she gasped, her pussy sloppy from the strokes. "Yesss!"

"Who pussy is this?" Love growled, feeling guilty, but at the same time feeling a need to assert his dominance.

"Make it yours, daddy! Make it yours. Show me you can make it yours!"

Love was trying to do just that. He spread her ass cheeks, giving him total access to deeper penetration, long dicking fast and furiously, making her pussy smack with moist friction.

"Oh fuck! I'm about to cum," she moaned as she bucked back wildly. Using her inner muscles like a suction cup, Love's strokes got caught up in the sensation. He pushed himself deep inside of her and exploded.

"Damn!" she gasped. "You tryin' to turn me out?"

"Tryin?" he quipped cockily, and then they both laughed.

"I'ma make this dick part of the job description," he added.
Jazmine adjusted her skirt as she turned around. She put on
her glasses and replied, "Be careful what you ask for,
sweetie."

\* \* \* \* \* \*

"Oh! Lil' Joe, who fadin' that!" Swag barked later on that
night as he, Gotti, and their team shot craps.
"Nigguh, fifty on that!"
"Fuck that. Put fifty over here. I'm ridin' wit' Swag!"
"Straight money, nigguh. Let them shits ride!"
They talked shit back and forth as bet and side bets littered
the ground with twenties, fifties, and big faces. Swag hiked up
his sag as he bent over smoothly shaking the dice.
"Four-four bulldog shit!" he grunted as he released the
dice.
They landed on five.
"Double down, yo. This nigguh 'bout to crap!" Gotti
yelled, urging his man to put down more on the side bet.
"Nigguh, you crazy as fuck. Put fifty over here." Swag
laughed, dice sounding like ice in his grip.
He let them go with a gangsta snap that sounded like the
crack of a small caliber.
Four.
Swag looked at Gotti and winked.
"Stick wit' me, nigguh. I'ma take you places. But for now,
I'm just gonna take your money," Swag cracked and Gotti
laughed.
They were on 'the block,' acting like the trap was theirs,
which it seemed to be. On all four corners were the lookouts
along with shooters on the roof of the building on both ends of
the block. The fiends were in a frenzy because they had almost
doubled the size of the double up. Shit was flowing like water.
"Gotti! Boy, is you crazy?"

voice was shrill like the twanging of a copper wire. .   ·ew turned to see that a purple Escalade sitting on 24's and pipe striped with white, was double parked. The person driving was the source of the voice. From a distance, late at night or pissy drunk, she was a brown-skinned bombshell. Amazonish in height, but petitely proportioned in size. She wore her hair in a long pink Mohawk that she draped over her shoulder and hung to her chest. Everything she wore was Versace. Her nails were perfect and her strut was fierce. She had her shit together. The only problem was she was a He.

His name was Miss Toni, a transsexual hustler that kept his ear to the ground and kept a team of homos, bi's, and tri's that got money for him. He was also a friend of Gotti's.

"Yo, Toni. Fuck you talkin' about?" Gotti questioned, vexed to be interrupted, especially because he was losing.

"Boy, you know I heard what you done did out here! What's wrong wit' you! Love ain't dead. You just been misled. Chill! He rockin' you to sleep!" Toni warned with dramatic flare.

Gotti spat to the side while holding his dick.

"Man, fuck that pussy!"

"Pussy he may be, but some pussy's *burn*, baby," Toni shot back.

Swag chuckled, amused by Toni's wit. The sound made Toni look in his direction.

She had to do a double take.

"Gotdamn! Who this fine motherfucka here?"

Swag smiled.

"Swag, yo."

"Swag?" Toni echoed, looking him up and down admiringly. Then a look came across his face and he frowned. "Swag? Not the hell raisin' Swag I been hearin' of, by any chance?"

Swag shrugged. "Could be."

"No offense, honey, but how this lil' nigguh 'posed to push up on killers?"

"'Pends on what you mean by little," Swag quipped, grabbing his dick and Toni saw the large print in his jeans.

She had to fan herself.

"Lord ha' mercy. Mother needs, chile. Gotdamn, mother *needs*."

"Yo, fall back," Gotti cut in, a little too firmly. "Swag don't get down like that. Do you, fam'?" Gotti questioned, his tone sounding like a taunt.

"Oh, straight, huh? So is spaghetti 'til it gets heated up." Toni winked.

"Toni, get to the gotdamn point. You see I'm tryin' to get this money," Gotti said, referring to the money scattered on the ground.

Toni looked at the money with disdain and replied, "Nigguh, fuck that short money. I'm talkin' *real* money. Now, you know I fuck wit' Love. He *always* do mother right. But I fuck wit' you even more 'cause you do mother *more* than right," Toni purred, touching Gotti's chest. "So if you in the business, I'm buyin'. But the numbers gotta be good and the shit right. Now, if the answer is yes, then let's take this ride and the drinks are on me."

Gotti knew Miss Toni spent big money, so he was definitely ready to take that ride. Besides, Miss Toni was . . . a friend.

"Shit, say no more," Gotti replied, scooping up his money. "Let's ride."

As he walked away, he glanced back at Swag with a taunting leer. "You coming?"

Swag smirked and gave him the finger.

# S W A G

Gotti laughed, but as Swag watched them pull away, the picture became crystal clear.

# Chapter Thirteen

When Swag pulled up on his bike in front of the little apartment he had rented to stash Rain in, she was standing outside, arms folded and foot tapping looking absolutely edible in her capri jeans, midriff top, and sandals.

Swag tipped this helmet back on this head.

"What you waitin' on? The bus?" Swag quipped sarcastically.

"Yeah, and you the goddamn bus driver. Don't get off the bike, 'cause you takin' me out," Rain retorted.

"Yo, Rain. I'm tired as fuck. I—"

"I'm tired too, Swag! I'm tired of being cooped up in that fuckin' apartment. I don't know no damn body around here! So . . ." Her voice trailed off with sass as she reached for the second helmet.

Swag grabbed her wrist.

"Have you forgot *why* you cooped up in that apartment in a neighborhood you don't know?"

With neck on swivel, she shot back, "I ain't scared. Are you?"

Swag smirked.

"Come on, daddy. I need to *breathe*. I know this reggae club in the cut. Nobody'll see us. You know if you don't do this, I'ma be a bitch." She pouted, purposely trying to play on his sentiment. "Besides, I'm safe if I'm with you, right?"

Swag flexed his jaw as if he was aggravated, but he was really amused.

"Get on the fuckin' bike."

Rain smirked, put on the helmet, and got on the back. Before Swag dropped his helmet back on, she kissed him on the cheek.

The reggae club was named Love People II and was a city and a half away from the apartment. It was near the docks and was housed in a large warehouse. It sat so close to the river you could smell the raw sewage. The spot was definitely in the cut. It was more like a bar with a dance floor than a full fledge club and was peopled by bad men and rude bwoys. Dreads everywhere, along with winding hipped, big body gals. Swag knew he was in a thug club when there were no bouncers or metal detectors. The smell of ganja straight from the bush filled the air and made seeing in the red-lighted club a task because of the thick wall of smoke.

Red, bloodshot eyes peered through jungles of dreads as Rain and Swag made their way to the packed dance area. The selector threw on a dub plate featuring Sean Paul and Ninja Man. Exclusive! The driving pound of the bass had already taken possession of Rain's body. She moved like she was made to dance. Swag just did his two-step.

The selector took the crowd through a classic set starting with Shabba Rank's "Bedroom Bully" to Terror Fabulous' "Action." He ran through a Super Cat dub of "Ghetto Red Hot" then dropped the needle on "Murder She Wrote". By the time he eased off with Mad Cobra's "Flex", Rain's body glowed like black gold from the glistening sweat, and Swag's two-step had evolved to reveal he could dance. His rhythm matched hers, almost mirrored it. She was impressed by the way he moved, impressed and intrigued.

After the club, they went to a nearby IHOP.

"I can tell you had fun tonight," Rain remarked over her pancakes.

Swag shrugged like, "It was ai'ight."

"It's okay to have fun. Gangstas can have fun too, you know?"

Swag chuckled. "Who said I was a gangsta?" he replied, drinking his orange juice.

Rain played in her eggs.

"So why'd you leave Boston?"

He took a bite of his sausage.

"'Cause I had to kill this nosy girl that asked too many questions," he joked.

"Funny, nigguh," she retorted, sourly. "I'm serious. I wanna know."

"Long story."

"Lies usually are."

"Naw, lies can be short, like . . . I love you," Swag said, holding back a smile.

Rain sighed hard.

"Like . . . really, Swag? Can I *ever* get a straight answer out of you? Why it always gotta be hoops wit' you? I *really* wanna fuck wit' you. But on this mystery shit, I never see you but in flashes. And when we talk, it ain't even talkin'. You think I'm *scared*, like I need you to protect me? Nigguh please! If that's the case, I'll walk out the door now."

"Well, there go the door right there," he replied cockily, looking her in the eyes, calling her bluff.

Rain glared at him for a moment, and then got up to leave. As she passed him, he grabbed her wrist.

"Sit down," he told her without looking up at her.

Rain looked down at him without moving. Swag looked up at her.

"I gotta repeat myself?" he asked calmly, but firmly. He knew Rain was a down ass chick, one he had plans for. Just, not yet. But she had forced his hand. A fact he accepted, but didn't appreciate.

Rain sucked her teeth and sat back down. Swag rested his elbows on the table and pushed his plate aside.

"Put it like this. Shit got hot for me back home, so I had to migrate, ai'ight? And the reason I never lay my head in one place is because a movin' target is hard to hit. Dig, Rain. This shit is deeper than you think, 'cause I go harder than you know. I can own this fuckin' city if I move right. No mistakes allowed, feel me? I wanna fuck wit' you too, but I need you to . . . not trust me, but trust your instincts," Swag explained, breaking the situation into digestible bits, and Rain swallowed.

"What you think got me this far?" She smirked. "Didn't I tell you I can see your future?"

"Yeah, well, sit back enjoy the ride and stop askin' so many damn questions then," Swag rebutted, only half-serious.

Rain stuck her fingers in her water and flicked water at him.

"Ai'ight." He chuckled.

"What you gonna do?" she taunted.

While they were having their lovers' quarrel, they had no idea a car full of shooters were speeding toward them.

\* \* \* \* \* \*

The shooters were launched by a phone call from Thump, who had received a call from scandalous ass Mona. She was fucking a married man who loved to eat at IHOP after their tryst. The spot was perfect because it was out of the way. Perfect for those who were on the creep, or simply didn't want to be seen in the city. Mona was the former while Swag and Rain were the latter.

Mona had spotted them as soon as they walked in. Her mind went ka-ching! And her phone went ring! She dialed Thump's number—no answer. She figured he didn't answer because he didn't recognize the number, so she texted:

Mona: *She Here!*

Seven seconds later, Thump called. "Yo!" he gruffed eagerly.

The married man cleared his throat. She held up an impatient finger. "She here. I see her right now! I'm at the IHOP out in the boonies," Mona said in rapid-fire fashion.

"Who she wit'?" Thump wanted to know.

"Some . . . dude. I ain't never seen him before."

*That's him!* Thump's gut told him. "Yo, take a pic of that nigguh."

"Boy, is you crazy! What if he see me?"

"Bitch, take the goddamn picture!"

Mona sucked her teeth and hung up.

"Ahhh, Mona," the married man interrupted.

"Nigguh, ain't you gotta call your wife or somethin'!" she huffed sassily.

He shut up. She snapped the flick and sent it to Thump.

Thump viewed the flick and saw Swag for the first time.

"I got yo bitch ass now!"

He called his young boy. "IHOP. Boonies. Now! Handle that!" As soon as he hung up, Mona called back.

"What!" he griped.

"You comin'?"

"Bitch, I can't fly! Yeah, I'm coming!"

"You got me, right?" she questioned with the anxiety of a money fiend.

"I said I did, didn't I?"

Click!

Mona glanced over at Rain. At one time, she and Rain were tight.

"Life's a bitch," Mona mumbled.

\* \* \* \* \* \*

The shooters were four-deep in an old Buick. The two men in the back were loading AK-47s.

"Ay, yo. I ain't shootin' no kids, man," the passenger protested nervously, cradling a riot pump shotgun.

"Nigguh, it's three in the mornin'. Ain't no kids out!" the driver shot back.

"This nigguh killed yo' cousin. Fuck you talkin' about!" the short dude in the back added.

"I still ain't killin' no kids," the passenger mumbled under his breath.

\* \* \* \* \* \*

"You ready?" Swag asked.

"Yeah," Rain replied.

They got up.

"Shit!" Mona cursed. She didn't want them to leave, not alive at least. It wasn't personal, just greed. She thought quickly.

"Be right back," she told the married man.

Mona approached just as Swag and Rain were at the cash register.

"Rain! Hey girl!" Mona called out.

Rain turned in her direction. Swag looked up. Mona gave Rain a hug.

"What's up, Mo? How you?" Rain greeted her cordially.

"You know me, girl. Stay slick and get it quick." She giggled, referring to a phrase they used to use when they hung together.

Rain snickered. "I know that's right."

Mona looked Swag up and down with a slow, deliberate scan.

"Uhh, who this, girl?"

"None ya," Rain shot back, half-joking.

Swag didn't believe in coincidence. Something wasn't right.

"Come on, ma. We out," he told Rain.

"Oh, my bad! I ain't tryin' to cock block, boo." Mona smiled, winking at Swag.

Swag gave her the stiff eyes as they walked out.

Mona watched. She had done all she could. The rest was on Thump.

"Who was that?" Swag asked Rain.

"This bitch from the club," Rain answered, rolling her eyes.

"I figured that," he replied as they got on the bike. Swag kick-started it.

"Why you figure—"

Before she got it out her mouth, the answer came barreling into the parking lot in the form of an old Buick.

"There they go!" the driver bassed.

Swag and Rain didn't even have time to put their helmets on. The first shot from the AK-47 narrowly missed Swag and shattered the IHOP window. Those inside screamed and ducked. Swag took off like a shotgun as a barrage of AK-47 and shotgun slugs erupted like a storm. Swag then turned the bike hard left and rated away in the same direction from where the Buick had just come, making the Buick U-turn and buying Swag a few seconds.

They hopped the curb, sparks flying as the bumper scraped the sidewalk, the whole time, busting shots. Swag gassed the bike, but had to break it back when a truck turned directly in his path. One shot even blew one of the truck's tires. Swag swerved and made his escape. The Buick was still hot and heavy. Swag leaned into a sharp right, and then just inside the block, he saw a U-Haul parked on the side of the street. He pulled the bike along the inside of the U-Haul, where it camouflaged him from the black street and turned off the headlight. He pulled out two .45s that were tucked in his back and handed them to Rain.

"Can you handle these?"

Rain sucked her teeth like the question was stupid, kicking off both safeties with her thumbs as an answer.

Within a blink of an eye, the Buick skidded around the corner.

"Where he go?" the driver bassed.

"Move this shit, yo! Go!" the shorter dude in the back urged him.

They thought Swag had already shot through the block. As soon as they passed the U-Haul, Swag pulled out behind the Buick. The hunted became the hunter.

Swag leaned closer to the handlebars as Rain braced herself with her thighs, and then let the twin calibers rip.

"What the fuck!" the driver sputtered as the first hail of bullets burst the back window.

Those were his last words.

Rain trained both guns almost barrel to barrel on the back of the driver's head. Had the shooter behind the driver stayed in place, the kill shot would've hit him in the shoulder and saved his life. But because he was twisting his body to aim the AK out the window, the shot whizzed by him and blew the driver's brains all over the dashboard and windshield. He fell forward, his jerking dead body making the steering wheel veer left.

"Fuck!" the passengers spat as the front passenger grabbed the wheel and snatched it back right. But he snatched it too far, just as they came barreling into the intersection. An SUV came from the left and plowed into the Buick, killing the shooter on the driver's side instantly. The other two would eventually slink away.

Swag broke the bike down, spun it around, and then disappeared from the scene of the crime.

# Chapter Fourteen

O nce they were safely back in the apartment, Rain wrapped her arms around Swag's neck.

"How I do, daddy?"

"Like a fuckin' trooper," he complimented her, giving her a strong, deep kiss. Then he added, "Now, let me make this phone call."

As Rain headed toward the bathroom, Swag thought about how well she handled herself. There were no jitters, no questions, which was a relief. Because had she shown any weakness, Swag wouldn't have hesitated to leave her leaking. He called Gotti.

"Yo'!" Gotti grunted in a tone that made Swag not even recognized his voice.

"G?" Swag questioned.

Gotti halted the blow job he was getting.

"Yeah, yeah, what up?"

"Yo, right now hit up that nigguh's club! Nigguh caught me slippin'. I ain't gonna front, but he missed. Show 'im we don't," Swag growled.

"Say no more," Gotti replied and hung up, preparing to get up.

\* \* \* \* \* \*

"Where you think you goin'?" Miss Toni asked Gotti.

"I gotta handle somethin'."

"What?"

"Deliver a message to Love at his club."

Miss Toni sucked his teeth.

"Is that all? Didn't I tell you I chose?"

With that, he grabbed his burner phone, dialed, and then spat rapid-fire instructions in Pig Latin. Within the next twenty minutes, two dyke broads with baldheads and tattooed necks would deliver the message to the club, killing the bouncer and three dudes in line.

Gotti tossed the phone on the floor.

"Now, where were we?"

*  *  *  *  *  *

Swag paced the floor, fuming because they had caught him slipping. He had no doubt in his mind that bitch at IHOP had something to do with it, but he wasn't sure. Not yet anyway.

Rain emerged from the bathroom, dripping wet and completely naked. Nipples hard, standing an inch off her chest. Her body was banging so hard the rhythm of her sexy was music in motion. Swag drank her in from head to toe, but his mind was elsewhere.

She grabbed at his dick, barely brushing it before Swag grabbed her wrist.

"Not now."

"Yes, now," she shot back, leaning in to kiss him.

He stepped away.

"Yo, what was that bitch name?"

"Mona, and it could've been worse."

"How you figure?"

"Because she woulda been one of the bitches you asked to put on the team," she answered, seeing the connection, too. Then she stepped up to him again and reached for him.

This time he grabbed both wrists.

"Didn't I say no?"

"Swag, I ain't tryin' to hear that shit! Everytime it's no wit' you, like really?"

He shrugged. "Your timin' fucked up."

"Timin'?" she echoed, putting her hands on her hips. "Anytime is the right time for *this* pussy!"

Swag laughed in her face. "Bitch, don't flatter yourself. Do I look like I should be pressed for pussy?"

"Naw, but you starting to look like a faggot!"

Swag snatched her up by the throat and slammed her against the wall.

She tried to loosen the grip, but couldn't.

"What the fuck you say?" he gritted.

"Just 'cause you can beat my ass don't mean you ain't gay."

Swag sneered in her face. "So now I'm a faggot, huh?"

"You tell me," Rain challenged.

He answered by running his tongue along the curve of her neck to the thick dollops of chocolate nipples, biting them just hard enough to make painful pressure squirt through her stomach and trip down her thighs. He lowered himself on his knees, putting her left foot on his shoulder. And he ran his tongue in and out of her pussy making Rain clutch the back of his head and fuck his face.

* * * * * *

The moment that Jazmine looked at Detective Hall, she sensed something was wrong. It was in the intense way he scrutinized her as he got out the car. They were meeting in their familiar spot, among the abandoned warehouses. Jazmine sipped her morning coffee as she leaned against her car.

Hall had a laptop in his grip and a manila envelope under his arm.

"Morning," Jazmine greeted.

"Mornin'," he grumbled back.

He opened the laptop on the hood of her car.

"What's going on, boss?" Jazmine asked, referring to the laptop and his state of mind.

He looked at her a moment, before replying, "This war is getting messier. Two more incidents, six more bodies, no more than an hour apart."

Jazmine nodded. "Thump already told me. He wants me to find out what the police know."

"What did you tell him?"

"Nothing yet. What should I tell him?"

Hall didn't answer. He turned to the laptop.

"Take a look at this."

When he clicked the screen, a grainy black and white surveillance video jumped on the screen. It was from the IHOP from the night before. Hall began it as the first shot shattered the window. He ran it back until Swag and Rain walked backward into the restaurant and to the counter where Mona approached them. When Swag looked at Mona, Hall paused the tape and zoomed in on Swag. Jazmine watched closely.

"The girl is definitely Haynes, and the guy is probably the target too."

"Motorcycle, just like McDonald's," Jazmine agreed.

"Exactly."

"So now we know what he looks like. Any luck on a name?"

Hall shook his head.

"Not yet. We're working on it. In the meantime, I want you to concentrate on finding out who that is through the street. The girl who approached them at the counter. She's a reliable source. Evidently, she knows the girl, him, or both. Find out," he instructed her, handing her a piece of paper with Mona's address.

"*Jagged Little Pill*." Jazmine chuckled.

"Huh?"

"Alanis Morissette, she's a singer. I was just thinking . . . never mind."

Hall grunted at the irrelevance and then pushed the laptop toward her.

"Take it with you. Study it. See what you see."

She nodded.

"And this, too," he added, handing her the manila envelope, maintaining eye contact.

The way in which he looked at her, Jazmine knew his tense vibe was tied to the envelope. Her gut balled up like a child into the fetal position out of fear."

"What is it?" she asked.

"Open it."

She did. She pulled out the picture of a female. One she knew well but had never met. A white girl, redhead, chubby face, sporting a confident smile.

Jazmine wanted to throw up. Her hands shook slightly. She had the distinct feeling of her face turning pale.

Hall watched, immensely enjoying her obvious discomfort. She looked up at him with weak eyes. A look he had never seen on her face. Gone was the confidence, the games, the manipulation, the sensuality, replaced by the gaze that resembled a starved beggar. The look made his dick hard.

"J-Jazmine," he began but couldn't muster any words. She knew she was caught.

"You're too young to outthink me, Georgia. Now, what do you want to tell me?"

Jazmine leaned against the car for support.

"James, please."

"Tell me!" he bellowed. The sound of his bass made her shudder.

Cornered, she realized her only hope was to tell him . . . everything.

# Chapter Fifteen

A slight drizzle, like the spray of sea mist at the shore peppered Thump's Caddy as he pulled up next to Love's BMW and got out. The moonless night cast no shadows, so Thump moved like one as he walked over to Love and gave him a pound. Right away, Thump sensed something different about Love. A subtle vibe of distance that Thump couldn't describe. But Love felt guilt everytime he saw Thump. His conscience whispered, "Nigguh, you ain't shit." But his ego would shoot back, "She chose, I didn't."

"What's up, fam'?" Thump inquired.

"I just finished hollerin' at Mousy's brother," Love said, referring to the bouncer that had gotten killed in the club shooting. "I told him we'd pay for the funeral."

"Word." Thump nodded in total agreement.

"Mousy was a good dude, yo. He ain't have shit to do wit' this bullshit," Love remarked.

"I'm sayin', yo. What can you do?"

"Indeed. We missed that nigguh again, and it cost us another soldier."

Thump didn't respond immediately because in a subtle way he felt the comment was directed at him. Like it was his fault.

"Yo, I told you let the wolves out, and I'ma have that nigguh head on some Dutch shit."

Love looked at Thump.

"Naw, fam'. I ain't sayin' you missed. I said *we* missed. We a team, right?"

Steady eye contact.

"Indeed."

Love looked away.

"I'm sayin', Love. I say we shut down shop for a minute and turn the heat all the way the fuck up. We been too worried about our gwop, but shit gettin' out of hand. Muthafuckas say it was two bald bitches!"

"Bald bitches? "

"You know exactly who sent them. That fuckin' faggot, Toni! Nigguhs formin' voltron 'cause they think it's safe. Fuck that! Shut the city down until we exterminate the problem!" Thump huffed, breaking it down like he was ghettocizing the art of war.

"Word up, fam'. I feel you, but yo . . . where you wanna be in five years?"

Thump scowled. "Five years? Alive?"

Love chuckled.

"I wanna be on a beach in Miami wit' a belly like yours," Love remarked, hitting Thump's big belly. "We done came a long way, yo. A long way . . . you know I'm throwin' a grip at this Mayor's election, right?"

"So?"

"So? Thump, man, you just don't know . . . the money in this city. We could triple our worth in five years! *Quadruple* it. And it would all be *legal*, yo."

"What that got to do with these nigguhs?" Thump probed.

"Everything. Maybe it's time we let this city work for us, instead of us workin' it, feel me?"

Jazmine's words slid from the back of his mind without prompting, and colored his thoughts of the moment. *Love may not be who you think he is . . .*

"What you tryin' to say, yo?" Thump asked.

"I ain't *tryin'* to say nothin'. I said it. We had a crazy run. Maybe it's time we fall back," Love replied.

Before Thump could answer, his phone buzzed a text. He looked at a picture of Jazmine, naked in the mirror, lying on the floor, leg's spread and cocked back.

Jazmine: *I Miss You . . .*

Thump was superstitious, so he felt like the text was some kind of sign, confirming the creeping sense of suspicion he didn't want to believe. Five seconds later, Love got a buzz from his cell phone. Thump had no reason to suspect anything, but Love did. Especially after he saw the picture. Something told him that Thump got the same message. The look on his face said it all. Guilt, anger, and arrogance filled Love.

*Did this bitch know we were together? Okay, she just playing games?* Love's thoughts grumbled. He tucked his phone.

"Just think about what I said, ai'ight?" Love urged.

"So what? We just let this nigguh go? Fuck Ant, fuck Mousy, fuck the family!"

Love shook his head like he pitied Thump for not understanding.

"Not at all. But it's more than one way to get this nigguh," Love proposed cryptically.

Thump didn't like the way that sounded. It made his honor bristle.

"The only way *I* know is the code, nigguh. Real talk."

The two friends parted, leaving something behind in the misty rain, something neither knew was gone. But when it was all said and done, it was obvious where it began.

\* \* \* \* \* \*

Jazmine hadn't known Thump and Love had been together, but she couldn't have planned it any better if she had. She sat on the bed naked, Indian style and opened the laptop. Although she tried to concentrate on the video, her mind kept going back to two words.

He knew.

He knew, and it threw more than a monkey wrench in her plan. She refocused, watching Mona in the lower corner of the screen talking to the married man. Saw when she spotted Swag and Rain walking in. Even though her back was to the camera, her body language was clear. The way she strained her neck to see around the plants obstructing her view. How she dialed the number, gave the married man the wait-a-minute finger . . . He knew.

*The Louisiana Superdome smelled like death, the heat stifling. She knew what the thirty-yard line looked like up close. She slept with her face on the number three. The sound of tortured whispers, the air heavy with despair, hate, confusion, fear. It was human nature at its worst. Human nature at its best, Katrina . . . .*

Just watching the screen, it was as if she could feel Mona's nervous energy. Left leg bouncing, checking her watch, continuously peeping as Swag and Rain sat talking to make sure they hadn't left. Rain got up to leave. Sat back down, and then exchanged more words with Swag. A few minutes later, laughter erupted from them both, oblivious to the presence of a snake on the other side of the plastic plants.

He knew . . . that Jazmine had been desperate. She had lost everything. Therefore, she had everything to gain. *The storm was both a blessing and a curse. It afforded her a chance to start over. Let the flood waters drown her past forever, who she had been, and what she had been becoming. The thought of being baptized in the water of broken levies, born again, free, made her laugh like she had already won.*

The footage showed Swag and Rain getting up. Mona is right on their heels. Hugs Rain. Rain's expression says she's really not feeling her. Swag looks her off. They leave. Mona watches them walk out. She spots the Buick entering the parking lot. She ducks even before the first shot is fired. A dead giveaway. That she knew.

He knew . . .

*The white girl hadn't moved in hours. The only reason Jazmine noticed her was the blood red hair, like roses framing her face. She clung to a pocketbook pressed to her chest. Several times, Jazmine's eyes wandered back to the white girl. It wasn't until the fly landed on her face that she knew she was dead. There was no remorse in her. New Orleans was submerged in death. Reeked of it. One more seemed more than nature; it seemed welcomed. Dead on the forty-third yard line. Jazmine went to her. She didn't conceal her deed. No one did. It was the worst of human nature. She rambled openly through her pocketbook. No money. No credit card, but she had a birth certificate and a social security card. That was better than money. It was new life.*

The screen went black, but she didn't notice it because she was back in New Orleans, and then her mind fast forwarded to Detective Hall. The look of triumph on his face when she told him the whole story. How she really wasn't Jazmine Coleman. The look was one of gloating. He knew he had her right where he wanted.

"I *own* you." He chuckled. "Every breath you take, thank *me* for it," he hissed.

Something about her made Hall want to possess her. Break her. It wasn't just the sex, it was *her*. She intrigued him to the point of obsession. Made him dig into her past and he struck gold.

"What are you going to do?" Jazmine asked timidly.

"I don't know. What are you going to do?" he shot back.

"Whatever you say," she answered without hesitation. She knew how the game was played.

He snickered.

"Smart girl."

Now, sitting naked Indian style on her bed, her stomach burned. Jazmine hated to be controlled. She had come too far to go back to that. Everything was lining up perfectly and now this.

*Kill him?*

That was always her first instinct, but she dismissed the thought. Killing a detective carried unintended consequences. But she had to do something . . .

And then it hit her.

Hit her with that energy of a thought so powerful, it made her get up and pace. Almost made her giddy with the simplicity of it all. She knew exactly what she had to do.

Jazmine rewound the tape and then zoomed in on Swag's face. She zoomed in so close and studied it so intensely. Jazmine could see her own face looking back at her through the reflection of the screen.

She looked focus.

"Now, I'll take care of you, mystery man."

# Chapter Sixteen

T he next day Swag got into Miss Toni's Escalade and shut the door. Miss Toni appraised him with a mixture of attraction and a disinterested curiosity.

"Gotti said you wanted to holla at me," Miss Toni said.

"I do. Drive," Swag replied.

"Forceful, I like, but demanding? Not at all," Miss Toni sassed.

Swag sighed like, "Ma, come on. Tomata, tomato, gimme the benefit of the doubt." He smirked, cracking a dimple.

"You lucky you got dimples," Miss Toni threw back, pulling off from the curb. "So what's up?"

"You."

"That's obvious."

Swag chuckled. "Then tell me why."

"Why what?" Miss Toni echoed, playing dumb.

Swag looked at him skeptically. Miss Toni knew he has referring to the hit on Love's club.

Miss Toni shrugged. "Call it a show of good faith. I know y'all nigguhs gonna win. Shit, Love been livin' off his rep and Thump's muscle for years. I'm a bitch wit' a dick and high heels, and I got more heart than half his crew."

Swag laughed.

"I'm serious." Miss Toni snickered, feminizing the esses.

"So, yo . . . what up wit' you and Gotti?" Swag asked, getting to the real point.

Miss Toni looked at him. "What he tell you?"

"I ain't ask him. I'm askin' you," Swag retorted.

"Then you need to ask him."

Swag nodded. "I guess that's my answer."

Miss Toni didn't respond.

"I'm sayin' . . . I just like to get to know the people I fuck wit' better, and you . . . I *definitely* want to know better," Swag stated, eyeing Miss Toni steadily.

Miss Toni looked him up and down and then squelched, "Beep! Beep!"

"Fuck is you doin'?"

"That's my bullshit detector. You in the red zone," Miss Toni quipped sourly.

"Naw, ma," Swag said smoothly, squeezing Miss Toni's thigh. "I'm dead ass."

The intensity of his touch melted Miss Toni's skepticism instantly.

"I thought you ain't cook spaghetti?"

"I guess we got a lot to learn about one another, huh?"

Miss Toni licked his lips. "What you tryin' to do?"

"Not right now. I got somethin' to handle, but believe me, I'ma be at you *ASAP*. Plus, I wanna make sure I ain't steppin' on no toes," Swag signified.

Miss Toni knew he was talking about Gotti. He held up one of his heavily jeweled hands.

"It may be a ring on my finger, but I bought that."

"That's what it is then. That's all I needed to hear," Swag replied, because indeed it was.

If Miss Toni and his team were going to be down with him, Swag didn't want his loyalty to Gotti alone. That would be a dangerous position for Swag to be in, so he had to even the playing field by any means.

Miss Toni pulled over.

"Don't make me wait too long," Miss Toni cooed, running a long fake nail tantalizingly along Swag's dick print, "'cause I will come get you."

"Trust me." Swag winked. "You won't have to." He got out and closed the door.

* * * * * *

"What's wrong, baby?" Jazmine asked that night, pulling her head from under the cover and taking Thump's dick out of her mouth.

She had been sucking his dick, but he was only semi-hard. She knew it wasn't her skills, so she knew something was wrong.

He caressed her cheek. "My bad, boo. Shit just crazy."

Jazmine slid up beside him.

"So talk to me."

He looked at her a moment, thought about it, and then replied, "Nobody is ever who you think they are. Now you tell me this bitch Mona is a fucking informant? Love on some other shit, like . . . I don't know."

Jazmine listened to him, and then asked, "Baby, tell me something. You ever think about being the boss?"

"I am a boss."

"I mean *thee* boss."

"Naw," he lied.

Jazmine giggled. "Liar."

He smirked. "I'm sayin'. . . . I don't know. We always been a team."

Jazmine sat up, playing with his stomach. "I'm just sayin', *you* should be the boss, especially if Love wants to do this politics thing. This is your shot," she urged.

The way he looked at her, she knew he was thinking about it.

"Shit would be sweet! You got me in place, keepin' all heat off the operation, and the streets *know* it's been you all the time, not Love. Why shouldn't you be boss?"

The thought had been crossing his mind since Love had been shying away from a war. It just wasn't in Thump to let it go. Every time he closed his eyes, he saw Ant's face. The fact that Love seemed okay with letting Ant die in vain made him question Love even more.

"You find out anything?"

Jazmine knew he was talking about Love.

"I'm on it, baby. Believe me."

He nodded.

"Listen, I've been thinking about this Mona chick. I know how you probably want to handle it, but let me handle it. Whoever this dude is, he smart, but I bet you she can lead us right to him," Jazmine proposed. "I'll kill him for you."

Thump looked at her, curiously. She was definitely a gangsta's wet dream. A killer with a badge on his payroll.

"You?"

Jazmine looked him in the eyes.

"Believe me, baby. I'm hungry too. I want you to see you got a ride or die chick fo' sho'."

Thump pulled her head down and kissed her passionately.

"You really down for a nigguh, huh?"

"*All* the way down." She smiled, and then down she went.

\* \* \* \* \* \*

The next day, Swag and Gotti sat at the table counting money while Rain sat on the couch braiding Renee's hair.

"Let me do that bitch, daddy," Rain volunteered.

"What bitch, Mama?" Renee wanted to know.

"What I tell you about that word, Né-Né?" Rain scolded.

Gotti laughed.

"She get it from you!"

"'Cept I'm grown, nigguh," Rain spat back. "Anyway, like I was sayin' . . . I can't *believe* that bitch tried to play me like that! This bitch tried to kill me! Oh, *hell* no! Daddy, I know exactly the rock that slimy bitch sleep under!"

"Ma, I know you in your feelings, but I told you this shit deeper than you think. They used her to get at us, so we gonna use her to get at them," Swag explained.

"Yeah, I'm feelin' that, 'cause you got a point. But when it's all said and done . . ."

"Be my guest."

"Fo' sho'!"

* * * * * *

Later that night, Thump took Jazmine to the strip club. He had to fight back his rage the minute he laid eyes on Mona. Jazmine sensed it, so she leaned over and said, "Be easy, baby. She gonna get hers. Trust me."

"Yeah," Thump gruffed, and then downed his drink.

Mona spotted them and sashayed over, full, juicy titties bouncing freely.

"Hey boo!" Mona greeted, leaning over and giving Thump a kiss on the cheek and then sat on his lap. "How are you doin'? Who's this? It ain't like you to bring sand to the beach," she cracked.

"I'm Jazmine."

"Yeah, yo. This is my lady. It's her birthday, but she ain't ever had a lap dance. I want you to break her in," Thump told her.

"Ooh, fresh meat, huh?" she teased, winking at Jazmine.

Jazmine giggled.

"This is for him more than me. I'm strictly dickly . . . except when I'm not feeling like myself."

"Well, shit, drink up!" Mona joked. She turned to Thump. "You know I got you, but ahh, you got somethin' for me?"

Thump wanted to say "yeah" and then put a bullet where her trifling brain was, but he choked it back and handed her a wad of money.

"That's three stacks, ai'ight?"

"I knew you was gangsta, boo." She giggled, and then got up and slid onto Jazmine's lap.

"You got some pretty ass lips," Mona whispered as she slowly gyrated on Jazmine. "Can I kiss 'em?" Mona asked seductively. She wanted to put on a good show for Thump.

Since Jazmine hesitated in answering, Mona leaned in to kiss her. When she was an inch away from Jazmine's lips, Jazmine said, "Instead of trying to fuck me, you should be fucking with me."

Mona stopped, leaning back a little. "I'm listenin'."

Jazmine knew she would.

"We missed the first time. We won't miss again. Help me make that happen, and you'll see double what you holding now."

Mona didn't have to think about it. She was with it. She cocked her head to the side. "Don't I know you from somewhere?"

"No." Jazmine smirked. "But you will."

# Chapter Seventeen

J azmine pulled up in the park, put on her sunglasses, and pulled her Atlanta Braves snapback low over her eyes. She didn't want to be recognized by the wrong people. As she walked through the crowd gathered around the baseball diamond, she heard the crack of an aluminum bat and the cheer of the crowd.

The softball game between the police department and the fire department was in play. She came because she knew Hall wouldn't be there.

"Hey, Coleman, izzat you?" a Polish officer asked as she walked by.

She stopped and flashed her social smile.

"Surprise, surprise."

"Long time, no see. Word is, you transferred across town," he stated with a tone of a question in his words.

Usually, if a woman was up and transferred, it was because of some kind of harassment. But Hall had only spread the rumor to add to her cover.

"Change of scenery. No big deal." She shrugged.

"Not from where I'm standin'," he flirted.

Jazmine chuckled lightly and walked off. She hadn't come to socialize. Jazmine was on a mission. She came to play a game. Simple psychology. If five people, at different times, tell a person they look sick, by the end of the day that person will think the same thing, or at least doubt they are healthy!

Her first mark was Detective Maston, at the top of the food chain in narcotics, right behind Detective Hall.

She said, "Have you seen Hall?"

He answered, "No. Why?"

"I'm worried about him. Does he seem . . . despondent to you?"

Maston shook his head. "Not really."

"I mean, I don't know. Maybe it's me, but it's like he's . . . distant. Just . . . not himself. I'm just worried about him, you know?"

Maston nodded. "I'll keep an eye on him."

Seed planted.

"I mean, shit, he's always moody." Another officer chuckled when Jazmine mentioned it to him.

"Well, more than usual." She giggled, "I mean . . . he's getting older, you know? And he really doesn't have anyone. That's gotta be hard going home to no one every night. I'm just worried about him."

Another nodding head, another seed planted. She made her rounds, planting a few more seeds, laying the trap and weaving the web, not of deception, of misperception.

\* \* \* \* \* \*

Since the club shooting, Love had begun to move with an entourage. He kept several shooters around him and a second car to trail him wherever he went. He even wore a vest.

A steady rain fell, giving the night a chilly air.

"So how we lookin' in the polls?" Love asked the person on the other end of his cell phone. He eased into the backseat of a beige Phantom. It pulled off.

"Your man says the union endorsement should put him over the top," Jazmine answered as she maneuvered her car through the rain.

"Does he think he can get it?" Love asked, with slight worry in his voice.

The councilman told me to assure you, he can. Don't worry, boo. He'll win," she told him.

Love chuckled.

"He better. I put a lotta gwop on his ass . . . But yo, speakin' of ass . . ."

"Not tonight, Love. Thump's expectin' me. I'll make it up to you."

"I bet you will," Love replied as he hung up.

He had fucked her several times, and with each nut, he felt less guilty and more spiteful. He was beginning to see Thump as a blind fool. His bitch was a slut. His judgment had to be sloppy. The thought only reinforced his thinking on it being time to get out of the game.

Love's team dropped him off at his mini mansion in the suburbs. Two shooters stayed with him. The other five went back to the city. Three of them branched off in separate directions. The last two went to a local sports bar and proceeded to get drunk while watching the UFC on the multiple screens. One of them, a lanky, light-skinned dude staggered off to the bathroom.

He stepped up to the urinal with a stumble, pulled out his dick and began to piss.

Someone grabbed him by the collar and pants and slung him into an open bathroom stall. He hit his head on the metal piping on the back of the toilet. Dazed, bruised, and drunk, he looked up and thought he saw two dudes, but he was only seeing one.

Swag.

He felt the cold barrel of Swag's Desert Eagle, and the feeling was instantly sobering.

"Yo!"

"Ssshh," Swag said, keeping his finger to his lips and backing up to shut the door. "Call Love," Swag demanded.

"I can't—I don't—I-I-I—" the dude stuttered.

Swag pulled out a phone and hit speed dial.

\* \* \* \* \* \*

Love was eating cold Chinese food straight out of the refrigerator, when his phone began ringing. He glanced at it and saw Ant's number. He froze mid-chew and felt anger rising along with his anxiety.

Swag listened to it ring over and over. He knew Love would answer, and he did.

"I see you still playin' silly ass games," Love hissed.

Swag put the phone to dude's mouth.

"Talk, nigguh. It's Love."

"Love?" dude slurred, fear pounding at his temples.

Love thought a moment. Then he said, "Yo, Benny. That you?"

Swag got on the phone.

"Naw, yo. It's us. You remember me, don't you?"

"So now I guess I'm 'posed to listen to you kill my man or somethin'?"

"I ain't gonna kill him. I just wanted you to know where I found him. Drunk." Swag chuckled. "Just like half your team right now. The other half fat and off point. You are slippin', Love. Shit gettin' too easy." Swag laughed.

Love flexed a jaw muscle. He took himself seriously, so he hated to be laughed at.

"But yo," Swag continued, "I'm sure they gonna cut this nigguh phone off soon, so I just wanted to give you a chance to holla while you still got the chance."

"Ain't shit to holla about."

"Yeah it is, yo. 'Cause we both know you don't want no war. You got too much to lose. Me? Nothin' at all. I'm hopeless, so therefore, so is the situation. Maybe we can find a way to work together," Swag offered.

Now it was Love's turn to laugh.

"Yeah, you think? Tell me where to meet you, so we can discuss it!"

"I'm dead ass, Love."

"Naw, nigguh. You just dead!"

"Maybe this conversation is a little premature, huh?"

"Naw, it shoulda just been aborted," Love shot back and hung up, vexed by Swag's audacity. Work together? He was so hot he was thinking like Thump. Fuck everything until Swag was dead. But that was the old way. The old him. The new him was on the verge of making millions legally, and he wasn't about to let everything throw shade on that. Still, something had to be done about this nigguh.

* * * * * *

A few nights later, Gotti and Mona ran into each other in Club Tru.

Both were looking for the other. The dance floor was tiled in black and white marble. It looked like a chessboard, and they resembled two pawns, both making their first move.

"Hey boo! Damn, you lookin' good. All buffed and shit," Mona flirted with a wink.

She remembered her powwow with Jazmine the day before, and how Jazmine said, "Whoever this Swag is, Gotti is how we gonna get at him. Thump says he acting like his right hand man."

"You know a nigguh go hard, ma. Come on, it's on me," Gotti replied as they made their way to the bar. He thought about what Swag had told him.

*"Thump got this bitch on a leash, so we gonna use that to get at him, feel me?"*

They got to the bar and Gotti ordered. The bartender brought the drinks.

Mona sipped.

"So what's up wit' you? How can I be down?" She giggled flirtatiously.

*"Bottom line, ma. You know the drill,"* Jazmine had said. *"I want the nigguh eating out of your hand."*

Gotti downed half his drink.

"That's crazy. I was just about to ask you the same thing," he shot back.

*"The best mark is always the one that thinks you the mark,"* Swag had reminded Gotti.

Gotti and Mona laughed at the coincidence. Her eyes said, "This nigguh don't know . . ."

His said, "That's what you think."

Their smiles were like the mutual bearing of fangs.

"So I guess we on the same page, huh?" Mona purred, pushing up closer on Gotti.

"No doubt."

*"We get this nigguh, he lead us right to Swag,"* Jazmine told her.

*"We get this bitch, Thump'll never see it comin',"* Swag told him.

Mona finished her drink. "I'm ready to go if you are."

"Then let's go."

\* \* \* \* \* \*

While Gotti and Mona were getting at one another, Jazmine was getting at Detective Hall's state of mind. She went to a bar that police favored near the docks. She spotted Detective Maston and approached him.

"Hey, Maston," she greeted him cheerfully.

"Coleman! Nice to see you again. How's the shit treating you?" He winked, referring to the precinct she was supposed to be transferred to, but he knew the truth.

She shrugged.

"Not as good as the ninety. Beer?"

"You buyin'?" He chuckled.

"'Pends on what I get for it," she flirted playfully.

"I would love to, believe me. But I've got an ol' lady who really admires Loraina Bobbitt."

They laughed. She brought the beers. Police talk ensued. Jazmine steered the conversation to Hall.

"How's the old man?"

Maston scratched his chin. "I don't know. Maybe you were right. He does seem a little more crankier than usual . . . distant."

Jazmine concealed the smile on the inside of her lips.

"I really feel bad for him. He was like a father to me," she said, using the past tense 'was', but Maston didn't notice it.

She laid her hand on his shoulder.

"Maybe you should try to talk to him," she said, adding in her mind, *So we can plant the seed in him, too.*

"You think?"

"I do."

He nodded. "I think I will."

* * * * * *

Later that night, she showed up on Hall's doorstep. He answered in his robe with a scowl on his face until he saw who it was. Then he looked worried and ushered her in.

"You should've called before you came. I would've met you on the spot," Hall told her as he closed the door.

"It's almost two in the morning. No one saw me."

"Still, it's risky."

"I like risk," she purred, wrapping her arms around his neck.

He smelled the alcohol on her breath.

"You're drunk."

"And horny." She giggled, although she wasn't anywhere near as drunk as he thought. "And I missed you." She tried to kiss him, but he pulled back and unclasped her arms like a chain from his neck, stepping away.

"Don't try and con me, Coleman, or should I say, Thomas."

Hearing her real name out loud after so long made her bristle within, but she struggled not to show it.

"We're still in this together, Larry. I may have . . . lied about *who* I am, but I didn't lie about *what* I am. I'm on your side," Jazmine stated, speaking with caution, like someone at gunpoint.

Hall snorted, watching her closely. Hall wasn't a dirty cop, but he didn't mind playing in the gray. He knew Jazmine was good at what she did, and now that he knew the truth, she couldn't switch sides because he'd keep a tight leash on her. Besides, if he took down Love's crew, the next time the chief of police's chair was vacant, he knew he'd be on the short list. Still, it was something about Jazmine that he just couldn't put his finger on, and therefore couldn't trust her.

"What are you after, Coleman?" he probed.

She looked him in the eyes and replied, "I want you to be chief so I can be a captain . . . until you retire. I'm ambitious and I'm greedy and I'm selfish, but I also want to make a difference."

She was telling the truth, just not the whole truth. He believed her. Satisfied, he took a deep breath and said, "Go home, Georgia. Your secret's safe with me . . . for now. Keep your nose clean and maybe I'll bury it."

Jazmine smiled, but inside she seethed. Maybe would never do.

"I'll be a perfect little angel." She winked, and then stepped toward the back hallway.

"Where you going?"

"Bathroom, wanna watch?"

Hall chuckled. Jazmine went to the bathroom. She peed. Washed her hands. Looked at herself in the mirror. After drying her hands, she stepped to the bathroom window. It wasn't large, but it was big enough. She flipped the latch, and then walked out. Hall was waiting by the door. She wrapped her arms around his waist.

"You sure you want me to go?" she quipped flirtatiously.

"I'm out of blue pills." He smirked.

She kissed her fingertips, put them to his lips, and then left.

# Chapter Eighteen

W hat up? You ready?" Swag questioned as he popped the clip in his AR-15.

"Yeah," Gotti grumbled with an undertone of aggravation.

"You ai'ight?" Swag probed.

Gotti turned and eyed him with a glance as tight as a vise grip.

"I said yeah, didn't I?"

Swag sensed it, but couldn't put his finger on the pulse of Gotti's attitude, but there was no time for that. It was time to get it in.

They were ready to move on the second hottest block in the city. The plan was for Swag and Gotti's team to hit the block up from opposite ends. They were in one van with three goons while the other half of the team was in another van. Both vans simultaneously mashed the gas and sped into the heart of the block. People were everywhere, fiends and hustlers alike. Swag and Gotti thought the block would fold easily.

They were wrong.

Thump had schooled his team well. They may have lost 'the block,' but they damn sure weren't about to lose this one. As soon as the vans skidded up, two sets of gunners emerged from the darkness on both sides of the street. Swag's people were taken by surprise. The gunfire sounded like an angry conversation spoken in bullets. Both sides came heavy, but Thump's people had the advantage because Swag underestimated them.

The first death was the driver of the van Swag was in. The bullet blew off the side of his face and twisted his face down on the passenger seat. His foot came off the brake and the van rolled into the parked car.

By this time, Swag and Gotti had bailed out the van and were having their say in this deadly conversation. Bullets flew and bodies dropped. Several of Swag's team, a few from Thump's, but the game changed when a bullet grazed Gotti across the shoulder.

"Gotdamn!" Gotti gritted as he fell against a park car, and then squatted for cover.

"Yo, G! G! You ai'ight!" Swag barked, banging back from his place of cover.

"I'm good. I'm hit though!" Gotti yelled back.

Nothing had gone as Swag had planned. He could see several members of his crew lying dead in the street. He let off one more round, and then he made his way back over to Gotti.

"Where you hit?" Swag asked.

"My shoulder. I'm good though! Keep it hot!"

"Naw, fuck that. We gone!" Swag countered.

Gotti didn't protest. Busting shots and duck walking, they made it back to the van. Swag opened the passenger door and the dead eyes of the driver looked him in the face. A shot rang out and shattered the windshield. Swag tried to shift the driver's dead weight but couldn't move him.

"Move!" Gotti barked, shoving him aside.

Gotti grabbed the body by the collar and then dragged him out of the way, dumping the body on the ground. He climbed in while Swag fired on Thump's team, and then jumped in.

"Go!" Swag bassed.

Gotti threw the van in reverse, got low, and began backing out, leaving the other van of dead shooters.

Swag kept it hot, busting out the window but staying low too. Two of Thump's people gave chase. Swag caught one in the face, stopping him dead in his tracks. He dropped and quivered.

Gotti screeched to a momentary stop, threw the van in drive, and then skidded off into the night.

\* \* \* \* \* \*

As soon as Swag and Gotti came through the door, Rain was on them.

"Oh my God! Gotti! You are bleedin'! What the fuck!" she exclaimed, hating to see her family covered in blood.

"I'm ai'ight, yo," Gotti grunted, even though he was losing a lot of blood.

He tried to take his shirt off but couldn't lift his bloody shoulder. Rain helped him take it off. Her eyes grew big at the gaping wound.

"Gotti, you gotta go to the hospital!"

He looked at her like she was crazy. "I can't go to no fuckin' hospital!" he spat.

"I'll sew it up," Swag said.

Rain and Gotti looked at him. Swag told Rain what he needed. She picked up Gotti's car keys, gave Swag a smack on the lips, and then headed for the door.

"And get some coke, too. Numb that shit up," Swag added.

"'Kay," Rain answered and then left.

When Swag turned his attention back to Gotti, he was taking off the top from a bottle of Absolute. He took a hard swig and then poured the rest on his wound. He growled deeply. It was like Swag could feel the sizzle of Gotti's flesh under the raw burn of the alcohol. When the searing pain finally subsided, Gotti bellowed, "Fuck! How the fuck we let them nigguhs eat us like that? Goddamn!"

Gotti was in beast mode. He hated to lose.

"I lost half my team in one goddamn night!"

"We slipped, yo. We underestimated them nigguhs," Swag surmised.

Gotti glared at him. "Naw, nigguh, you slipped! I thought you scoped this shit!"

"Fuck you mean, *I* slipped!"

Gotti approached him.

"Just like the fuck I said!" Gotti bassed, bare barrel chest heaving, bloody and sweaty.

Swag could see where this was headed, but he could also see there was something deeper going on.

"Look, yo. I know shit is fucked up. Seein' your mans and them hit up like that, but goddamn, we ain't gonna get nowhere beefin' wit' each other," Swag reasoned.

Satisfied that Swag had backed down, Gotti fell back a step.

"How that shit feeling now?" Swag asked, referring to his shoulder, and trying to change the subject.

"Like I got shot," Gotti shot back sarcastically.

Swag shook his head with a chuckle.

"Don't start actin' like you give a fuck now, nigguh," Gotti mumbled.

Vexed by the unnamed tension in the air, Swag spat, "Ay, yo. What the fuck is wrong wit' you? All I asked was how the fuck you doin, Gotti."

Gotti gritted on him. Silently sizing him up, he then said, "What you think? I don't know? Huh? You thought he wouldn't tell me?"

When Gotti said 'he', Swag knew exactly who he was talking about.

"Look, yo." Swag sighed. "I asked the nigguh what was up, and he gave me the green light. I ain't know it was that serious."

"You don't get it, do you?"

"Get what?"

Gotti slowly approach. "Word up. You gonna try and play me like that?" he said, voice calm . . . too calm.

It was in the flinch of his neck muscle as he launched the massive left. Swag saw the blow like it had been telegraphed, dipping it easily. He started to launch a blow of his own, but Gotti's left arm backtracked after missing its target but grabbed Swag by the throat forcing him to the wall. Gotti had hands like mitts and a grip like a constricting boa. Swag tried to struggle free, but he was immobilized from the neck up.

"You thought you was gonna play me!" Gotti barked, tightening his grip. "I know you knew what's up . . . how I felt. I know you knew," Gotti added, leaning in closer, until like a magnet to metal, he kissed Swag dead in the mouth.

At first Swag froze. He thought about how Gotti had looked at him the first time he laid eyes on him, the way he woke up and found Gotti watching him sleep. The way he teased him around Miss Toni, and it all made sense then . . .

Swag relaxed. He pulled Gotti's body to his and slid his tongue in his mouth. The receptive response sparked Gotti, and he snaked his tongue around Swag's greedy tongue. Pressing his body against Swag's, he felt Swag's bulletproof vest.

"Why you always wear that shit?" Gotti asked before kissing him again and grabbing his ass, marveling at its softness.

"Yo, chill . . . you know Rain about to come back," Swag reminded him, pulling back.

Almost on cue, they heard Rain pull up in Gotti's Maxima.

Gotti reluctantly backed away. The heat and the passion of the moment made him forget about the pain. He gripped his hard dick, lustfully.

"Goddamn, yo," Gotti swore, licking his lips, "this shit isn't over."

Swag simply smiled.

\* \* \* \* \* \*

A week later, Jazmine made her move.

She didn't drive. She took a cab to a nearby park. Dressed in sweats and sneakers, Jazmine looked like any jogger getting in an after-work workout. She jogged the two blocks to Hall's house and jogged right into the backyard. From there she sidled up alongside the house until she was directly under the bathroom window. She got on her tippy toes to slide the window up all the way, and then used a trashcan to boost herself through it. It was a tight fit, but she shimmied through like a woman shimmied out of a tight dress. Jazmine put her hands on the toilet, and then the floor, until she could get her whole body inside.

Once inside, she quickly shut the window and checked her thin leather gloves to make sure they hadn't been ripped in the process. They hadn't. She stepped out of the bathroom and headed upstairs to the bedroom.

Jazmine knew she had plenty of time before Hall came home, but she still didn't want to waste a minute. She began going through drawers, careful not to leave any evidence that the place had been rummaged through. She smiled at the irony that it was a police academy that had taught her how to commit untraceable crimes.

"Isn't it ironic?" she sang in a playful voice, not unlike Alanis.

Ten minutes later, she found it. The manila envelope with the incriminating evidence was in the sock drawer, out of sight, but not hidden. This simple fact showed he had underestimated how far she was willing to go to keep her secret.

Or maybe, she was underestimating him?

Maybe this wasn't the only copy. A sobering thought, but one she'd have to live with. Jazmine checked her watch. It was time. She slid under the left side of the bed, closest to the closet and the only chair in the room. She shoved aside a few shoeboxes, some old papers, and waited.

Forty minutes later, Hall shut the front door with a solid thud and a grunt. He wore his exhaustion like a coat. It wasn't a physical exhaustion; it was a mental one, a confusion that became too persistent to fight.

It had all begun a few weeks back, when a few of his colleagues began to ask, "You okay, detective?"

In the beginning it was simple enough, but after a while the question started to sound like, "You're not okay, detective." Concern seemed to become condemnation, which sparked his resentment, and in turn, his resentment was used as justification for the compensation. A vicious cycle. He was old, he was alone and lonely. He was depressed, defensive, aggravated. It was exhausting to keep up with.

As he ate and watched *Jeopardy* as he did every night. "What is a Higgs Boson?" answered one of the contestants. Hall thought to himself, *Am I depressed?*

Had he been alone for so long that he forgot what depression was? Was he numb? Was that why he craved Jazmine's company? Wanted to possess her? Why he had dug into her life and found the key to do just that, but now that he had it, he felt guilty. Like he had violated her. But what was she running from? Who was she hiding from?

Maybe he was depressed. Maybe he was lonely, or maybe his reality was simply being manipulated. He finished his dinner and went upstairs. He went into his bedroom and instantly thought of Jazmine.

The thought was so strong, he thought he smelled a hint of her cocoa-mango scented body wash in the air. He took off the holster and slung it over the chair by the closet. Disrobed, laid his clothes in the chair, and then took a shower.

Twenty minutes later, he came back in the bedroom and cut off the light. He lay down on the right side of the bed with a relaxing sigh, taking the weight of the day off his tired feet.

Had he looked at his holster, he would've known it was empty. But the room was dark, his mind was tired, and his eyes were closed. He drifted, drifted, closer to sleep, lying on his back as if afloat. At first he didn't even feel the steel of the gun barrel, but when she cocked the hammer, his eyes opened instantly. He froze, disoriented, until he heard, "Sshh, don't move. It'll all be over in a minute." Jazmine's voice somehow relaxed him. Somewhere in the back of his mind, he was glad this wasn't a random break-in. It gave the moment meaning.

And then it made sense. This wasn't a murder, or at least it wouldn't look like one.

"Cold-blooded bitch," he said in a deadpan manner.

"Still mean it as a compliment?"

*Boom!*

And he was gone. Brains and blood sprayed the alarm clock and lamp. Jazmine took the gun and placed it in Hall's hand, trigger finger interlaced with the trigger ring. She laid the arm at the right angle, stepped back and took a look at the scene. There was no need for a suicide note. She had already written it in the minds of the precinct weeks ago.

Jazmine looked into his dead open eyes staring up into nothing, and felt a twinge of guilt.

## ANGEL SANTOS

"I wish you wouldn't have got in the way, Larry," was her eulogy, as she took her secret out of the house and back into obscurity.

# Chapter Nineteen

I mean, I knew he was depressed, but I definitely didn't expect *this*", "I saw him comin', but what can you do?" "Maybe if I just could've talked to him . . ." These were the kinds of things Jazmine heard as she moved through the funeral home where Larry Hall's wake was being held. They say the murderer always returns to the scene of the crime. In Jazmine's case it was true. She felt like everything had gone down smoothly, but she came to make sure.

But she was only half right.

"Coleman, how you doing? How you holding out?" Detective Maston inquired as he gave a warm friendly hug.

"I'm . . . here, you know?" Jazmine answered, plastering her face with a stoic expression appropriate for the moment.

Maston nodded. "I still can't believe it," he remarked, shaking his head.

"I know. I'm still trying to process it all."

The conversation lapsed for a moment. Jazmine knew that Maston would probably be the next chief narcotics detective, so she was trying to feel him out.

"Listen, Coleman. I've kinda inherited Hall's workload for the time being."

"I couldn't think of a better man for the job considering…"

Maston smiled a tight smile. "Thanks. But the thing is, I see a lot of things that I'm not comfortable with."

Her stomach tightened. "Like?"

"I think you know," he replied, looking her in the eyes. "The fact that you weren't really transferred is number one."

"Yes, I know, and as soon as time permits, I wanted to speak with you about that. We've really made a lot of headway in—" Jazmine explained, talking fast.

He held up his hand. "This is neither the time nor the place, Coleman. But as soon as . . . Soon, there will be changes," he told her firmly.

Jazmine tried to reply, but someone else had already taken Maston and his attention away. She cursed under her breath, and then glanced around to make sure no one heard her. She knew exactly what Maston was referring to. The undercover operation.

She had gotten rid of one problem, only to create another. Briefly, she glanced at the framed picture of a smiling Hall on top of the coffin. To her, the smile looked like he was mocking her. He had gotten the last laugh.

Jazmine saw her plan going down the drain. She bided her time until she saw Maston leaving. She cut through the crowd and left out behind him, catching him at his car, halfway down the block.

"Detective!" she called out as she approached, walking as fast as she could in heels without losing her swag.

He turned and waited.

"I was wondering if I could have a word with you."

"If it's about what I think, there's no need. My mind's made up."

Jazmine smiled politely with a hint of mischievousness.

"You haven't even heard my side. How about a drink? It's on me. Again."

# SWAG

"I'm late for my daughter's play," he replied without returning her smile.

"Play, huh?" She smirked, letting the pun play on his ears.

Maston's patience was wearing thin. "Coleman, I don't know what kind of . . . *arrangement* you and Detective Hall had, but I can assure you that option is no longer on the table. Your undercover assignment will be terminated. End of story. You're inexperienced, and as Hall says in his notes, reckless. Case closed."

Maston was like the holy cross to Jazmine's vampiric ways. He was the type Jazmine hated: A good man, the kind immune to her poison.

"Fine," Jazmine said tightly, stepping back so he could get in his car.

"And Coleman, that's effective immediately. I may be only the acting chief now, but if I were you, I'd play the odds, you know? Let's make an attempt to co-exist. You follow?"

Jazmine totally understood.

"Whatever you say . . . boss," she sniped.

Maston got in and drove away, leaving her to juggle the ticking time bomb he had just tossed at her life.

\* \* \* \* \* \*

The next morning, Swag came to Gotti's apartment bright and early. He had to knock three times before Gotti finally stumbled to the door, looked out, and then opened it.

"Yo, what up?" Gotti asked groggily, wearing nothing but his boxers and a morning erection.

Swag glanced at his dick, smirked, and replied, "You."

Gotti took a subconscious step back.

"Yo, you buggin'. You know I got shorty here."

Swag smirked and winked.

"Of course I do. That's why I'm here."

139

Swag headed for Gotti's bedroom and entered without knocking. Mona was naked from the waist up, only covered by a sheet from the waist down.

"Yo, what up, ma? My turn?" Swag joked, walking toward her while reaching for his zipper.

"Please!" She rolled her eyes. "I don't *even* get down like that."

"I know that's right." Swag laughed, adding, "Nah, but for real. I'm glad you here. It's my b-day, yo."

"Happy Birthday, boo."

"No doubt, we plan on gettin' it in tonight, and I know you know some bad ass broads. Bring 'em to my spot," Swag told her.

Mona had a good poker face, but she was cutting flips inside. Here was her target inviting her to his spot. She wanted to call Thump on the spot, but she knew the nigguh would come soon enough.

"Oh, don't worry about that, boo. Let Mona hook you up. I got you." She winked.

"I bet you do." Swag chuckled and walked out.

He brushed past Gotti, who had been standing by the door with his back to Mona. He blew Gotti a kiss as he brushed past and left.

# Chapter Twenty

L ife was good. Love's club was packed, which meant the gwop was rolling in. Not to mention the momentum in the streets was turning back in his direction, because with the election of Joyner to the mayor's office, he now had a new weapon in his arsenal.

The election hadn't even been close. Joyner had rode the wave of Love's money to a landslide victory. Joyner was the new mayor-elect, which made Love a king maker, because he had Joyner in his pocket.

Looking out over the crowd from his perch in VIP, Love felt a surge of power so potent it almost made his dick hard. No one in the club gave a fuck who the mayor was, so they didn't pay attention to the election. All they knew was Love had made champagne free for the night.

"What I tell you, my nigguh? Didn't I tell you we was gonna win!" Love laughed, reaching across the table and giving Thump dap.

They were basking in the light of their success. Love on one side of the booth, two of his henchmen on his back, eyes peeled, while Thump and Jazmine occupied the other side of the booth.

"Yeah, yo," Thump admitted with a grin. "Yeah, you did. I ain't gonna front. I ain't think you could pull it off."

Love laughed.

"I told you, fam'. Politics is just like the streets. You get the right connect, lock the right blocs, and boom! You the mac wit' the cheese," he bragged, and then cut his eyes at Jazmine. "Ma, looks like the door is wide open to move you up all city."

"Naw, I'm good," Jazmine replied with a tone that turned up its nose at Love.

Love eyed her as she sat up under Thump like she was all about him. Like she hadn't been sucking Love's dick as well. But as of late, she hadn't been returning his calls, turning him down when he pushed up on her at the office, and now, giving him nothing but attitude. It was like she had cut him off cold. It threw Love off balance, like she knew it would. It was only a matter of time until he blew his cool.

Thump sensed it too. All night she had been frosty toward Love. Thump liked it, but didn't know where it had come from all of a sudden.

"To each his own, right?" Love remarked with a smirk, but underneath he was hot. He turned back to Thump.

"What up wit' that other thing?"

Thump checked his watch.

"Any time now. The bitch told me the nigguh invited her to his birthday party. Soon as he call her, she gonna call me."

Loved nodded. "Gotdamn, that's buzzard luck. Die on your birthday!"

He and Thump laughed.

"And plus, we massacred them nigguhs, yo. They came through and got ripped! I sent a team through the block, and them nigguhs wasn't even out!" Thump reported, feeling amped that the tides had turned.

"That's what's up. We get this nigguh and be done wit' this bullshit. We got bigger fish to fry."

One of Love's team members approached the table, bottle of Ace of Spades in hand.

"Yo, Love. What up? This shit dead. Let's hit up that new strip club 'cross town. I heard that shit is bonkers!"

"Strip club?" Love echoed. "Nigguh, this *is* a strip club if I want it to be!"

The dude laughed.

"Yo, you buggin', Love!"

"Word?" Love smirked arrogantly, and then turned to one of his henchman. "Ay, yo, come here."

The henchmen neared, and Love whispered in his ear. He nodded and then walked off.

"Watch this," Love snickered, looking from face to face, stopping on Jazmine, as if the statement was really directed at her.

A few minutes later, the DJ announced wildly, "Ay yo, peep this! Love tryin' to make one of you sexy ladies five thousand dollars richer! He said whoever got the sexiest strip tease and baddest body is walkin' outta here wit' five stacks, bottom line! And y'all know the god about that gwop!"

Indeed, they all knew. So when the DJ threw on the Luke classic "Doo Doo Brown", the club went bananas. True to his word, Love had turned the club into a strip club as most of the chicks turned into instant strippers, shimmying out of dresses, dropping jeans, raising skirts, all in the hopes of hitting the jackpot. Even some chicks in VIP had joined the frenzy.

Love's whole crew, including Thump, were laughing and enjoying the spectacle of human nature. Love looked at Jazmine with a look that said 'I can do anything. Choose wisely'. It was a look that flaunted his power, but Jazmine knew it was she who had the power, because she had made him feel the need to prove his. She communicated this with a sour smirk and a subtle shake of her head.

That was all it took. The subtleness of her rejection infuriated him, and he lashed out, masking his venom with humor. "What up, ma? I'm sure you know the drill."

At first, Thump wasn't sure he had heard what he thought he did.

Jazmine instantly stood up with feigned indignation.

"Nigguh, what you just say?" she spat.

The laughter at the table stopped like it had fallen off a cliff. Despite the blasting music all around them, along with the cacophony of voices and laughter, their table was bubbled in its own silence.

"Yo, Jaz, sit down. Hol' up," Thump told her and she did.

Then Thump looked at Love. "Yo, bro. What up? You gonna disrespect my lady like that?"

Even though Love knew he was out of line, his pride had him locked in. He shrugged it off arrogantly. "Believe me, fam'. It ain't that serious."

"It ain't serious? Nigguh, you disrespect me, and it ain't serious?" Thump stressed, his temperature slowly building.

"Yo, Thump. Chill, fam'. Nigguh ain't mean nothin'," one of the team members said.

Thump ice grilled him and then turned back to Love.

"Thump, word up? You serious? What? You want me to apologize to your lady or somethin'? This your lady? You sure?" With every question, Love's tone and pitch grew to an ominous crescendo.

Thump glanced at Jazmine, feeling a knot in his stomach. Something was telling him to let it go. But his pride had him locked in, too.

"What you mean, am I sure? Nigguh, what you sayin'?"

"Come on, Thump. Don't tell me you really feelin' this broad," Love intoned, looking his old friend in the eyes, willing him the strength to recognize game.

# SWAG

"Yo, Love, man. I'm askin' you what you sayin'," Thump repeated more calmly but just as intensely.

"Ai'ight, you wanna know? Man, I been fuckin' this b—"

Thump's reaction was almost like a spasm, involuntary. As soon as the truth came out of Love's mouth, Thump jumped across the table trying to shove the words right back down his throat.

Love's truth instantly crushed the truth Thump wanted to believe, and all he knew was to react physically. He swung on Love, but so many bodies intervened, he ended up hitting someone else. He grabbed Love's chain, and as they pulled them apart, the chain broke but no one noticed.

The commotion drew attention quickly. The music dead. The dancing ceased. Smiles were swallowed. All eyes gazed up at VIP.

"The fuck is wrong wit' you!" Love barked, being restrained by one of his henchmen. "You gonna swing on me over a bitch!"

"Nigguh, fuck you!" Thump hurled back, being restrained by three bodies.

"Yo, Thump, for real? For real!" Love was hot, but his guilt kept him from really being angry. In his mind, he was doing Thump a favor, even though he was doing it for a selfish reason. But as they say, "It's the thought that counts."

Thump and Love glared at each other across a divide greater than the simple space between them. Both knew nothing would be the same, but both were too caught up in the moment to give a fuck.

Thump took Jazmine by the arm and gritted, "Let's go." Still gripping her arm, he guided her toward the main office and then down the back fire escape.

Jazmine remained silent throughout the tussle, letting it play itself out.

She had been goading Love with her coldness, knowing his pride would crack like a thin sheet of ice, and it couldn't have come at a better time. The bomb was still ticking.

When she and Thump got to the bottom of the fire escape, he jerked her around and forced her against the wall.

"You fucked that nigguh, didn't you? Didn't you!"

Conjuring up tears like a spell, she looked into his eyes and gasped, "I can't believe you would ask me that! Oh my god! You *believe* him!"

Thump gripped her by her hair and forced her head back, jabbing his finger in her face.

"Bitch, don't try and play me! Did you fuck him?"

"Deon, you're hurting me!" she cried.

"I'ma kill you if you don't answer me!"

"Then kill me! Do it! I can't believe you! I can't believe you'd listen to that bullshit!" She sobbed. Jazmine snatched away from him.

"You don't know me. You don't know me at all if all it takes to question what we have is the word of a jealous ass nigguh! You know what? I'm glad he said it, because now I know what you really think about me."

With that, she turned and started to walk away.

Thump stood, watching the love of his life walk away. He was at war with himself. Why would Love have to lie? Why would he say he fucked her if he hadn't? But on the other hand, she had been cold toward Love all night. She wouldn't act like that if she was fucking him. Would she? His heart and head battled, but the fact that she was walking away forced his hand.

"Jazmine!"

She took a few more steps and then stopped. Slowly, he caught up.

"I'm not sayin' I believe him. I'm just sayin' I don't know what the fuck is goin' on."

"That ain't good enough, Deon. I need a man that believes in me like I believe in him. I have never given you a reason to doubt me, so don't let somebody else's word make you doubt me," she gamed, with wet cheeks and anguish in her voice.

Before Thump could respond, his phone rang. Relieved for the interruption, he answered, "Yo . . . yeah."

He hung up and bit his bottom lip with aggression. Jazmine knew it was bad news.

"What is it, baby?"

Thump looked at her, fire in his eyes.

"They missed."

# Chapter Twenty-One

E verything was going according to plan.

"Yo, Mona, you ready?" Gotti asked over the phone.

"As ever," Mona cooed as she drove, her car packed with four of the baddest chicks from the club.

"Ai'ight. Well, check it. We over on First. You know the complex on the corner? We the last apartment. Apartment 3C, got me?"

"No doubt. I got you," she confirmed, and then hung up.

Without missing a beat, she hit Thump's team.

"Yo."

"Follow me. He on First."

"Yep."

Click.

Behind her was a van with seven shooters and a sedan with four more. They were bringing their big guns because Thump felt like he could end this shit once and for all. So he sent in his heavy hitters.

Mona turned the music up, snapping her fingers and shimmying in her seat. The only thing on her mind was how she was going to spend the ten grand Thump had promised her. The plan was simple enough. Lead the shooters to the spot, take the girls in, and then get somewhere and get low. Not all of the girls, just her. The other girls had no idea they were bait. That fact didn't bother Mona at all. They were strippers at the same club, so they were her competition as well. If something was to happen to them—then more money for her.

As she pulled into the complex, the sounds of the music and female chatter filled the car. Mona checked her rearview mirror and watched the van and sedan dead their headlights and stop near the entrance off to the side.

She pulled up to apartment 3C, checked herself in the rearview, and then the five chicks got out, loud and ghetto, like a pussy riot.

Mona rang the bell. The door opened, but she didn't see who opened it, a fact she didn't pay attention to until it was too late. The chicks all stepped in. Gotti, who was behind the door, shut it behind them. Mona's eyes grew big, wondering why he was wearing a gas mask over his nose and mouth. Before she could mention it, he gripped her by the neck and put the nine to her head.

"Shut the fuck up and come on!" Gotti barked, sounding like Darth Vader through the mask.

One girl started to scream, but Gotti backhanded her with the pistol, knocking her out. A mercy, seeing as what was to come.

"Lie down! Now?" he commanded, and they didn't hesitate to comply.

"Gotti, I—" Mona started to beg, but he squeezed the words right out of her throat.

"Shut up!"

He led her quickly to the back door, and then shut it behind him. The girls lying on the floor started to get up, but the shooters kicked the door in, guns ready to blaze.

"Yo, what the fuck!" the lead gunner growled. "Where they at?" he asked the girls.

They all pointed to the back door.

"What's that smell?" he questioned.

Gotti half-pulled and half-dragged Mona through the darkness to Rain waiting in his car.

"Triflin' *bitch*!" Rain spat as she punched Mona in the face so hard she thought she broke her own hand.

Mona's nose shot blood and her knees buckled. Rain snatched her by the collar and stuffed her in the backseat before jumping in behind her.

That's when Gotti heard the crack of the front door being kicked in. Shit was happening too fast. He jumped in the driver's seat and simultaneously leaned down, flicked his lighter and set aflame the thick trail of gas that snaked back to the apartment. He mashed the gas before he even shut the door because there was no time to waste. He snatched the gas mask off and through the rearview mirror, watched the trail of fire race for the apartment.

\* \* \* \* \* \*

*What's that smell?* That was the thought that entered the lead shooter's mind. It was faint, but pungent. The type of smell you only catch every other breath. Then he heard the screech of Gotti's tires. He ran toward the back door and that's when he saw it.

Fire.

It took his mind a nanosecond to process the fire in the backyard swiftly approaching them, and in that nanosecond his mind made the connection between the fire and the smell.

"Gas!" he yelled, as he shot past the stove with all its pilots on and had been for a few hours, filling the house with pure butane.

The rest of his crew didn't make the connection right away. But it didn't matter, because it was already too late. Because once the flame slid under the door . . .

*Kaboom!*

The force of the blast killed the four girls and four shooters inside instantly. It blew out the neighboring apartment, killing a couple in the midst of making love to Luther Vandross. It blew out parked car windows and set off car alarms. The rest of the team was blown back, disoriented and totally unprepared for the two baldheaded dykes to come running up from their safe position near the entrance and mowing them down spraying bullets like a firefighter spraying water, leaving the whole team wet from blood. The two silent killers disappeared just as quickly as they appeared. The only one to survive was the driver of the sedan. The blast had made him deaf in his left ear. He jumped out of the smoking car and staggered off. He was the one that called Thump.

"Yo, I don't . . . fuckin' fire, man! The whole apartment," he stuttered into the phone.

\* \* \* \* \* \*

When Gotti was half a block away, he saw the mushrooming inferno over the houses in his rearview mirror. He smiled. Swag had been right. The shit had worked like a charm. Gotti speed dialed his number. No answer. He frowned and started to dial again, but before he could, his phone rang.

"Done?" Swag asked as soon as Gotti answered.

"Done."

"Put the bitch on the phone."

Gotti tossed the phone in the back to Rain, who had been steady beating Mona bloody. Mona's whole face was swollen. Rain was trying to beat her to death.

"Yo, Rain. Chill. We still need that bitch," Swag said on the phone.

Hearing Swag's voice brought her out of her zone, reluctantly. She picked up the phone off the floor and said, "Daddy! You promised I could do this bitch!"

"Chill, ma. Put her on the phone."

Rain sucked her teeth and put the phone to Mona's bruised ear. She flinched. When he heard her labored breathing, Swag hissed, "A bitch ain't been born that can take me fast, you hear me?"

She nodded as if he could see her. In the background, Mona heard a sizzle. Static? Echo?

"Now check, I'm the only reason you alive. Play fair and you'll stay that way, you understand?"

"I . . . I'll do what . . . ever."

"Call Thump. Tell him it wasn't your fault. Tell him you want your money. When you meet him, we'll be right there. Understood?"

"Okay . . . when?"

"Now. Put ma on the phone."

Rain got on the phone.

"Let her go."

"Daddy, you sure? The bitch ain't gonna do nothin' but jump the fence!"

"You heard me. Let her go!"

He hung up.

Rain glared at Mona's bludgeoned face. She wanted to kill the bitch so bad, it hurt. But her loyalty was stronger than her blood lust.

"Gotti, stop the car."

He didn't ask any questions. He pulled over. Rain got out and snatched Mona out by her hair, dumping her on the curb.

"Bitch, for once in your life, you better do right, or—" Rain hissed and then kicked Mona in the mouth so hard she spat out a tooth and collapsed on the pavement.

Rain got in and gritted. "Drive."

Gotti lurched off.

Mona lay on the concrete, her whole being in intense pain, but not as intense as the relief she felt for still being alive. In the time of the moment anybody with a soul would've turned their life over to God. But Mona didn't have one. All she thought about was getting her money from Thump and leaving town. There was no way she was going to help Swag set Thump up. That was out of the question. Swag must've been crazy if he thought she'd do it. But she just didn't understand the method to Swag's madness.

She sat up and slowly, painfully, struggled to her feet. Once she stood, she wobbled like a drunk, and then staggered off.

# Chapter Twenty-Two

I ... I've never seen anything like it . . . these drug boys are turning our city into . . . into a war zone. Turning the city into Syria," the fire chief said before walking off from the camera's angle.

The female reporter, with the apartment fire being fought behind her, added," Chief Minelli has said it all. This certainly looks like a war zone.

"Several are dead, a few from gunshots. Police are incensed, as—"

Thump snapped the TV off, seething, and then just stared at his reflection in the black screen. He heard the shower cut off in the bathroom. A few minutes later, Jazmine came out naked, drying her hair with a towel and tossed her phone on the bed.

"I tried the bitch three times. Still no answer," she announced.

Thump looked at her.

"They blew the joint . . . fuckin' blew it up," Thump said, as if he couldn't believe it himself.

"Wow!" Jazmine remarked, shaking her head. "I guess we underestimated him."

Thump began pacing the floor.

"How the fuck he knew?" he grumped, shaking his head.

As if on cue, his phone rang. He checked it. Mona. He looked at Jazmine.

"This that bitch now," he told her.

"Where the fuck you been?" he spat into the phone.

"Thump, it wasn't my fault! Gotti snatched me up as soon as I walked in! It was like they were waitin' for me!" Mona slurred.

"What the fuck are you eatin'?" Thump asked, barely able to understand the words coming out of her swollen lips.

"My mouth is fucked up," Mona replied, tears beginning to fall.

Thump and Jazmine's eyes met. He looked vexed.

"What?" Jazmine asked.

"Where you at, yo?" Thump asked.

"'Cross town."

"Let me see the phone," Jazmine told him. He handed her the phone. "What happened, Mona?"

Mona told her the story, slurring and all. Her tears turned into sobs.

"They said they'd kill me if I ain't help them set Thump up."

"Set Thump up?" Jazmine repeated, looking at him.

"Who gonna set me up?" Thump paused.

Jazmine held up a finger.

"What you say?"

"I said hell no!"

Jazmine smirked.

"You said hell no and they let you go?"

Mona recalled how she sounded.

"I mean, I told them yeah, 'cause they was gonna kill me! But I ain't mean that shit."

Jazmine didn't respond.

"Hello?" Mona said.

"Where are you?" Jazmine asked.

Mona heard the accusation in Jazmine's voice. Felt it in her gut. The fear shook her.

"I swear, yo. I ain't have nothin' to do wit' this," she swore, missing the irony. After all the lies she had ever said, now that she was telling the truth, nobody was buying it.

"I know, shug. We good. I'm just gonna bring you your money." Jazmine smiled, her accent always more pronounced when she got devilish.

"I'll umm. Okay. I'll . . . call you back," Mona stuttered and then hung up. Her plans had just changed by half. Now she was just going to get out of town.

Jazmine handed Thump back the phone.

"That's how she knew. The bitch set us up!"

"I knew I shouldn't have trusted that bitch! Fuck I listen to you for?" he huffed.

"Oh, now you gonna blame me!"

"You the one said use her!"

Jazmine took a deep breath.

"Look, baby, we don't have time for the blame game. We in this together, okay? I told you this fuckin' detective is putting me back on *traffic* duty, so we have to move now! We gotta hit this nigguh, and not to mention, figure out where we at with Love."

Thump bristled at the sound of the name.

"What about Love?"

"What you gonna do about him?"

"Do? Look, I ain't thinkin' about that shit right now. We'll work it out," he replied.

"What if you don't?" Jazmine pressed. "Then what? Love changes, Thump changes, and best friends become strangers sometimes, you know? Maybe you ought to start thinking like a boss."

# S W A G

From the look on his face, she could tell he already was.

\* \* \* \* \* \*

Two days later, Miss Toni threw a birthday party for himself at a gay club called The Pink Diamond. The interior was set off by pink halogen lights that curiously made everything look light fuchsia. The club was packed with boys and girls, but the girls were boys and the boys were girls. Boys danced with boys and the girls danced with girls.

Swag slid through with Rain on his arm. The scene fit him like a glove; he was in the element because he straddled the line so well. Rain held on to him, looking around with a strange expression on her face.

"Daddy, these people crazy . . . confused like a motherfucka," she remarked. Yet, even she didn't know who she was walking with.

They took a booth in the cut. As soon as they got comfortable, the two baldheaded dykes slid in the booth, one on either side of them. The one next to Rain stuck out her long, lizard-like tongue and rolled it like a wave. "Ello, love," she greeted her in a thick British accent smeared all over Jamaican Patois. "Wha gwaen she? Oonu love cocoa."

Rain looked her up and down and then replied, "Daddy, you betta get this bitch if you want her."

Swag chuckled, shaking his head at the girl. She shrugged and slid away with her partner.

"Damn, we must be the only straight people here," Rain remarked.

"You think?" Swag quipped.

Rain looked at him.

"And don't think you over, nigguh. I'm still hot wit' you."

"Ma, don't sweat it. I know you cut like that, but these hands too pretty to get blood on 'em," Swag crooned, taking her hand in his and kissing it.

She was referring to Mona's death. The day after the inferno, her body was found in her shower, water still running, eyes still open, her brains decorating the wall behind her lifeless head, courtesy of three shots from Swag's .40 caliber.

Rain looked around the club once more, skeptically.

"Daddy, you sure you wanna fuck with these freaky muthafuckas?"

Swag shrugged.

"Why you think no gay drug ring ever been busted?"

"'Cause they janky!"

He laughed. "That too. But for more, it's 'cause the world scared to see 'em. They right there in your face, and you still can't see 'em. Like they say: You can't stop what you can't see."

"I still don't like 'em."

"Don't knock it 'til you try it."

"No thank you."

"I know that's right. I'll be right back," Swag said when he spotted Miss Toni.

He rose from the booth and made his way through the crowd.

Miss Toni was talking to someone, so Swag tapped him on the shoulder. He turned around, all smiles.

"Happy Birthday to me!"

"So what, I don't get a birthday hug?" Swag remarked.

Miss Toni gave him a hug.

"Oh, you can get it all right," Miss Toni said as they broke the hug. "Problem is, seems like you want what I want."

Swag chuckled.

"Too much peanut butter and not enough jam," Miss Toni added, looked at Swag's crotch and concluded, "what a waste."

"But we can still do business, right?"

"My second favorite subject."

Swag looked around and then said, "I want you to holla at Love."

"Love?" Miss Toni echoed, but caught on quick. "About…"

Swag could tell by his tone he understood, so he smiled because he liked smart people.

"You already know. You can't get money and bust guns at the same time. Maybe we can work somethin' out."

Miss Toni nodded and sipped his drink.

"Makes sense."

"Especially now that we got the upper hand. It's always good to call for a truce when you winnin'. It saves the other nigguh's face from surrenderin', feel me?"

"Fo' sho'. When you want me to get at him?"

"Give it a few days. Let this shit sink in . . . Give him time to consider the alternatives."

Miss Toni looked at him. "You sharp for a Boston nigguh."

Swag laughed. "You sound like a Yankee fan."

"Anything wit' a big bat, shug," Miss Toni shot back, adding, "just make sho' you call me to jam whenever you tired of being the peanut butter."

"No doubt," Swag responded as he watched Miss Toni sashay away. When he looked up, Gotti had him pinned from across the room with a jealous gaze. Swag, pretending not to see it, turned and walked away.

# Chapter Twenty-Three

J azmine knocked on the open door of what used to be Hall's office, but was now Maston's. She stood in the doorway in uniform and a helmet under her arm.

"You wanted to see me?" Jazmine asked, poker face in place, her tone banal. Maston looked up from his computer.

"Yeah, I did . . . for the last two days. What took you so long?"

"Had a lot of tickets to write," she replied sarcastically, but without sarcasm in her tone.

He smirked knowingly.

"I'm sure. Come in."

She stepped forward a few paces until she occupied the space between the desk and door, surrounded by boxes she knew contained Hall's personals.

"Have a seat."

"I'd rather stand."

Maston eyed her curiously, trying to figure out what was askew. It wasn't bitchy coldness. No. It was the fact that, deprived of her sexuality, she was powerless. Because he was beyond the reach of her voodoo. She was like a panther that had been de-clawed, de-toothed, and knew it. He felt secure in the thought.

"Suit yourself. Anyway, I need you to brief me on Hall's operation."

"Isn't it in his files?"

"Most of it. But I'd like your input as well. Is that a problem?"

Jazmine looked at him a moment, and then responded, "There's a new crew in town, run by some guy named Swag. He's behind several murders, including the McDonald's shooting, and I believe the apartment bombing last week."

Maston jotted down a few notes. He sat back and sighed.

"So we've got a war on our hands?"

"Two."

"How so?"

"Love and his second in command, they call him Thump."

"Deon Stokes," he said, letting her know he was familiar with the name.

"I was in the midst of turning Stokes against Love and priming him to turn on him as well."

"You turned him against Love? How?"

Jazmine paused before answering. The subtlest hint of a smile crossed her lips.

"The same way Helen turned Troy."

Maston coughed to stifle his chuckle.

"So . . . how far did you get?"

"Not far enough."

"What about mayor-elect Joyner? You hinted to Hall that Love may be involved with his campaign. Anything concrete?" he asked.

"That was a dead end," she lied.

He nodded.

"Okay, anything else I need to know?"

"You're making a mistake," she replied.

"Duly noted. But I meant about the investigation. We are on the same page, right? You do know that it's over, correct?"

"I think you made that clear already, detective."

"Then why did you go to Stokes' apartment last night?"

He dropped the bomb on Jazmine so swiftly, and without warning, it took all of her skills not to show her anxiety.

"You're following me now?" she quizzed, indignation rising in her voice.

"Apparently, I needed to, considering," he answered, eyeing her reaction.

"Look, detective, I have to live in this city still. I entered into this investigation at Hall's request because I was determined to see it through. Now, by taking me off the case, you've jeopardized my well being, so I needed to tie up the loose ends," she explained.

"I see. Would you like if I transferred you out of this district?"

"No. Everything's fine now."

He watched her for a moment.

"Okay."

"One last thing, detective."

"Yes?"

"This isn't over," she told him, her gaze crouched and locked on his.

He chuckled. "Are you challenging me, Coleman? Because if I were you, I wouldn't do that."

She shrugged. "You're not me," she replied. Then she turned and walked out, leaving Maston to wonder what she could possibly have up her sleeve.

Jazmine went straight to the bathroom. She gripped the sink, weak in the knees. Maston had followed her. He couldn't have seen anything. But the point was she had gotten lax. She looked at her reflection in the mirror.

"You're slipping," she warned herself.

She had gotten too arrogant. Although she was seven steps ahead, she knew all it took was a stumble to fall. She took a deep breath, rolled her neck, and then put on her mirrored sunglasses and looked in the mirror again.

"Tighten up," she told herself. "We almost home."

\* \* \* \* \* \*

Mayor-elect Joyner was on top of the world. He had won the city by a landslide victory. He had several deals lined up for his construction company as a result of his election, and he had a date with a super model for the night.

Joyner chirped the alarm of his 2011 Buick Regal, thinking to himself, it was time to upgrade. His thoughts were filled with Benzes, BMWs, and Jaguars as he started to pull out, but he was stopped short as a police motorcycle swooped in and stopped alongside the front of his car blocking him in. He watched the officer get off the bike, noticing it was a female. She walked up to the car. He lowered his window.

"Good afternoon, officer. Did I—"

Jazmine took off her mirrored sunglasses and smiled.

"Remember me, Mr. Mayor?"

It took him a slight second to flip through the rolodex of pretty faces in his mind. When he hit on a match, he mentally did a double take.

"You!"

Jazmine smiled.

"Exactly, that's me. Love's office? His receptionist? Cop? You beginning to see the picture yet?"

Joyner's mouth was stuck agape. Jazmine was tempted to reach in and shut it. Instead, she continued.

"Let me help you then. I'm a cop, obviously. I was a cop when I met you and passed messages between you and Love and shuffled money . . ." She then added, "Now you know what I know, and we *both* know if anyone else knew then that could be a real problem for the mayor-elect."

Recovering, Joyner cleared his throat.

"I-I have no idea what you're talking about," he stuttered.

"I figured that," Jazmine responded, reaching in her pocket and pulling out an iPhone. She dropped it in his lap. "Ourlittlesecret.com. It's a website I made for just me and you. Use the password: Oops." She giggled. "O-o-p-s. Listen and then I'm sure you'll remember."

Joyner looked down at the iPhone like it was a dead rat.

"Tell Love, if *I* go down, *he's* going down!"

"You're right, so why don't *you* tell him. He doesn't know I'm a cop, but I'm sure you're going to tell him, right? Tell him I said hi and it was fun. You can remember that, can't you?"

He looked at her, trying to wrap his mind around her approach.

"Don't hurt yourself, shug. Just play your position. You tell Love I said it's either him or you. You got me?" she quipped, and then put her sunglasses back on. "Personally, he'd rather it be him, because I've got a feelin' you and I can find common ground. Oh, congratulations."

Jazmine got on her bike and pulled off.

# Chapter Twenty-Four

L ove couldn't believe his ears.
      That night, he and Joyner met in a cemetery. Love just looked at Joyner.

"Didn't you hear me? I said the bitch is a cop!" Joyner repeated with fervor.

Love lunged at Joyner, catching him off guard. Love pinned Joyner to the side of a tree.

"Man, what the—"

Love was oblivious to his protest. He snatched open Joyner's suit jacket, and then ripped open Joyner's shirt, sending buttons flying.

"Drop your pants," Love said, seething inside.

"Nigguh, are you crazy? Look at my goddamn shirt!"

Love snatched a .45 from his waist and put it to Joyner's forehead.

"Drop your goddamn pants!"

Joyner dropped them.

"Happy now? I'm not wearing a fucking wire. I ain't the police! She is!"

Satisfied, Love slowly re-tucked the gun and began to pace the area back and forth, back and forth.

Joyner pulled up his pants, examined his shirt, and gritted.

"Tell me again what she said," Love told him.

"She said she was a cop and she knew about—the situation. I looked at and listened to her website. It's all there," Joyner informed Love, shaking his head.

Love was enraged. He and his crew had never been infiltrated. The police had failed repeatedly to get on the inside, and now, one woman had done what a legion of police had failed to do. She had got in and divided the leadership.

His thoughts turned to Thump. *Did he know?* Love shook his head. He didn't even want to think the thought, but it crept right back. Hadn't Thump been acting crazy over this chick? Hadn't he flipped on him, his own man, over her? If she could make him do that, what else could she make him do?

Joyner stood watching Love, petrified. He cursed himself for being so stupid as to get in bed with gangstas, but his greed overruled his stupidity.

Being mayor of a major city was a jackpot for the savvy operator, and he considered himself the savviest. Now he didn't know if he'd even make it out of the cemetery alive. Ironic.

"Love, listen." He spoke slowly and calmly. "If she wanted to bust us, we'd already be busted. The way she set this up— she can be bought. The question is, how much is it gonna cost us?"

"You just figurin' that out?" Love shot back. "Sometimes a dirty cop is worst than a clean one. They can never be bought, but you always get sold."

As if on cue, the phone Jazmine had given Joyner rung. Joyner pulled it out of his pocket, looked at it, and then at Love.

"It's her!" Joyner said nervously, like a kid just spotted by his mother.

"Why am I not surprised," Love replied.

# S W A G

Joyner started to answer it.

"Don't," Love cautioned. "Gimme your phone."

Joyner started to protest, but then remembered the last time. He handed Love his phone from his other pocket. By then the phone stopped ringing.

"What number she call from?" Love inquired.

"Uh . . . 555-3372."

Love dialed. Jazmine picked up first ring.

"I like the way you think," Jazmine said, "but don't worry, I wasn't tapping it."

"I'm sure your calling at this particular moment ain't a coincidence."

"Not at all, and you can thank the mayor for that. You could teach him a thing or two about losing a tail."

"Where are you?"

"Close," she replied.

"Why don't you come on over and we talk face to face," Love remarked, picturing himself sliding the barrel of the gun in her mouth like he used to slide his dick.

Jazmine laughed.

"You'd like that, wouldn't you? Not yet, shug. First, let's get an understanding."

"I'm all ears."

"All I want is an introduction to your connect."

Now it was Love who laughed.

"Bitch, suck a dick. I look like a rat to you?" Love spat.

"I see we're not on the same page, because you seem to think you have a choice," Jazmine replied with country silkiness. "So let me paint you a picture, baby. I could go to your connect. Say you turned on him. Maybe, he'd turn on you . . . maybe he kills you. Either way, you'd be out of a connect, or I could bust the mayor. He'd flip on you in a heartbeat. Look at him. You think he's shaking because he's cold?" She giggled. "Now you, on the other hand, could kill Mr. Mayor, but then I'd have you on murder one. *Or you could introduce me to your connect as your new partner, let me handle the dirty work, while you sit fat and play 'legit'.*"

*This bitch definitely slick*, Love thought. She was offering him his cake and a way to eat it, too. A clean break from the game with her, a cop, becoming his go-between. It was too good to be true, but too good to refuse. "Fifty-fifty," he stated.

"Seventy-thirty, no negotiations, Love. This isn't a deal. It's a debt," Jazmine responded.

Love's silence told her he agreed.

"What Thump know about this?"

She snickered, and then replied, "Ask him." Jazmine hung up.

Her words confirmed Love's worst fear. Thump knew. He could've been the one to mastermind the set up. That thought infuriated him. He tossed Joyner his phone.

"Well?" Joyner questioned anxiously.

Love looked at him with contempt.

"Nigguh, just take yo' dumb ass home," Love hissed.

"What about this?" Joyner asked, holding open his button less suit jacket and silk shirt. "This is a fifteen hundred dollars suit!"

"And I probably paid for it," Love replied without breaking stride and disappeared in the shadow of the trees.

\* \* \* \* \* \*

"Yo, Rain . . . Baby . . . yo chill, ai'ight. Let me explain!" Swag urged, hands up shoulder level.

Gotti was frozen beside Swag, an expression of pure astonishment on his face. Rain aimed the .45 with one tiny hand, and then gripped it with both hands. Stance squared, feet apart, braced for the shot she simply could will herself to let off. When one tear ran down her cheek, pausing by the corner of her mouth until her words allowed it to slide inside and she tasted the saltiness, is when Swag knew shit was real. He had on his vest, but she was aiming at his head.

As Rain stood there staring into his hypnotic green eyes, she wondered when she first knew the truth. Was it when she first introduced Swag and Gotti? The feeling she got when they laid eyes on each other made her feel like a third wheel, or was it the fact that Swag never sexed her? He would only eat her pussy, or when her daughter Renee even said, "Mama, he strange."

No, the truth was, Rain always sensed it in her gut, but she ignored it, hating to admit to herself that she had fallen in love with a homosexual. But she fought herself and decided to find out for sure, so she had told them she was going to the store. She had left, got in the car, and pulled off. But then she parked around the corner and walked back.

Purposely, she had left the door unlocked. A fact that, in their zeal to use the stolen moment her absence provided, had been overlooked.

When she threw open the door, her gut wrenched and she wanted to throw up seeing her cousin and her man lip-locked and feeling each other up with a freaky frisk.

Busted, they were both wide-eyed and stuck. Without hesitation, Rain grabbed the gun off the couch and aimed it at Swag's head. That's when he said, "Yo, Rain . . . baby . . . Yo, chill, ai'ight. Let me explain!"

"Explain what? That you's a fuckin' punk! Huh!" she shrieked, heartbroken as her temples pounded.

"Yo, cuz. I—" Gotti began, but she swung the gun in his direction and yelled, "Nigguh, shut the fuck up! I been knew about yo' freaky ass. But you? You was 'posed to be my man!"

Swag could tell if he made one false move or said the wrong thing, her emotions would pull the trigger.

"Ma, I'm sorry. I-I wanted to tell you, but I didn't know how. It's-it's who I am. Don't hold it against me. Please."

Rain steadied the gun, although she was trembling. Two tears fell from her chin.

"I should kill your ass."

"Please, ma. I'm sorry."

She shook her head.

"Yeah, you are. I can't believe this shit. I fuckin' loved your ass!" she shouted, choking back her sob.

"I'm sorry," Swag repeated, knowing how soothing the words were to her.

"From now on . . . we strictly business. You hear me? I put in work for this shit, too. Besides that, I don't fuck wit' you. You understand?"

"Yeah, ma. I understand," Swag agreed.

Rain eyed him hard and then tossed the gun back on the couch and turned for the door.

"Now you can do what the fuck you want!" she hissed, before walking out and slamming the door.

# Chapter Twenty-Five

I f you had a bird's eye view of the city, you would see the two cars of Love and Thump. Love, coming from the west and Thump from the east, headed directly at one another without even knowing it.

"The bitch is a cop."

When Thump heard Love's words, he didn't know how to respond. He knew he couldn't lie even if he wanted to, and he didn't want to. But to admit it seemed like an admission he just couldn't bring himself to make. He did the only thing left, he fronted dumb.

"What bitch?" he replied. But as soon as the words came out, they sounded lame and evasive.

For Love, Thump might as well have said he knew, because Love knew from the response that he did.

"How long you knew?"

"Yo, it ain't even like that."

"I ain't ask you what it's like. I asked when you *knew*?" Love emphasized with grit in his voice.

Thump bristled.

"And I'm *tellin'* you it wasn't like she a cop, yo. She under my wing."

"What the fuck is a cop? A cop is a cop, and you *knew* but *you* ain't tell me! That ain't a good look, Thump," Love cautioned him.

Thump knew he was in the wrong, but he also knew he wasn't a rat like it seemed Love was trying to say.

"So what you sayin', nigguh? You callin' me a rat or somethin'?"

"You said it. I didn't. All I asked is when you knew, and you still ain't answer! You tell me what's going on!" Love bassed.

Thump chuckled, but underneath he was beginning to boil.

"And this comin' from a nigguh that want the police on this team?" Thump accused, referring to Love's plan to play politics.

"Don't try and make this about me, yo. I told you what the deal was and where we goin'. Did you? Fuck no! You let a snake bitch slide inside, and now the bitch on us hard. Or should I say on *me*, hard!" Love shot back angrily.

"Ay, yo. This conversation is over because you need to get your head right before shit get ugly," Thump warned.

"Handle that bitch, yo. Or you right, it is gonna get ugly."

Love hung up.

Bird's eye view . . . headed straight for one another and they didn't even know it.

\* \* \* \* \* \*

Maston loved his wife.

They had been married eight years, two kids, five and eight. She was trying to start her own online business. They had a happy home and after eight years, they still had a fire sex life.

"Ooh, you feel so good, baby," his wife groaned as she rode him reverse cowgirl style.

Maston gripped her ass and drove himself in deeper, grinding her like he was stirring coffee.

"You like that?"

"Sssssss, I love it!" She trembled.

"I love you," he grunted, loving the sweet creaminess of her chocolate center.

He heard a series of car doors open without closing, but he didn't pay attention. That is, until he heard footsteps swishing through his grass, alongside his house and heading for the back, the sound of hushed voices audible.

Maston froze mid-stroke.

"What's wrong, ba—" his wife started to say, sensing the tension in his body.

"Sshhh!"

He urged her up and then got up behind her. He grabbed his boxers with one hand and his pistol with the other.

"Baby, is—"

"Wait *here*," he told her firmly. He stepped into his boxers as he walked, heading toward the door.

Maston took the stairs down two at a time. He peeped out the window and couldn't believe his eyes. The police had the house surrounded.

"Detective Maston! Come out slow, with your hands up!" a sergeant he knew by the name of Waltz, bellowed over the car's PA system.

His mind was totally boggled.

"Baby, what's going on?" his wife asked from the top of the stairs.

"I don't know," he answered sincerely.

Maston put his gun down and opened the door.

"Real slow, Maston!" the sergeant bellowed.

He had to be having a nightmare. He was a highly respected police detective, ten years on the force, but there he was being treated like a common criminal on his own porch. The police had three cars parked in a semi-circle in the street. An officer squatted behind opened doors, all guns aimed at him. Even a news van was on the scene filming everything.

"Get down on your knees, lace your fingers behind your head, and cross your feet at your ankles!" the sergeant's metallic voice instructed.

He obeyed. Three officers ran up on the porch, one cuffed him while the other two kept their guns on him.

"What the hell is going on?" Maston wanted to know.

"I don't know, detective. You tell me," one officer replied respectfully.

Several officers ran into his house while Maston was led to the back of a police car.

A few minutes later, his wife was escorted out in a robe and uncuffed. It took twenty minutes before he found out what had happened. His wife had called the police, saying that he had killed their kids and was trying to kill her. That's what the police had said.

Except, she hadn't.

The kids were tucked away in their beds asleep, until the police woke them up. His wife was furious.

"Do I look dead?" she screamed at the sergeant.

It was almost fifteen minutes before they took the cuffs off Maston. By this time, a second and third news camera had arrived. One reporter even asked, "Detective, why did you kill your wife?"

This was said while he was standing right next to her.

"Detective, I'm sorry. I don't know what the hell is going on," the sergeant apologized.

"That makes two of us," Maston replied, rubbing at the handcuff impressions on his wrist.

# S W A G

A crowd gathered and was being restrained by the police, and that's when he saw her at the edge of the crowd, looking at him smiling.

Jazmine.

Their eyes met. Hers, defiant and taunting. His, raging. Matson realized he had truly underestimated her. He wondered how she had set him up.

Had she hacked into his wife's cell phone? The police call center? The answer, which he would never know, was much simpler.

Technology was amazing. A feature available on most phones, is the ability to call someone and not only block your number, you can make it look like it's coming from another number entirely. That's all Jazmine had to do. She called 9-1-1, her number masked with Mrs. Maston's. She turned the TV playing the movie, *What's Love Got To Do With It* and said, "Oh my God! Oh my God! He killed my babies! My babies! P l e a s e! Help me! He's going to kill me!" She broke the connection, but the damage was done. The operator ran the number. Matson's address came up. The word went out, but once they realized it was a fellow officer, they came with fortified numbers.

There would be a story in the paper, and people in the precinct wondered if he had beat his wife regardless. It put a question mark by his name to replace Hall just as Jazmine knew it would.

The game had begun.

She blew him a kiss, got in the car, and pulled off.

\* \* \* \* \* \*

Thump was in his gambling spot playing cards. He hated to be disturbed when he was playing cards, but what his man told him made his ears perk.

"Gotti here. He said he needs to holla at you."

Thump forgot all about the flush he was trying to draw and replied, "Let him in."

A few moments later, Gotti was brought in, hands raised, at gunpoint.

The four other dudes at the table got quiet. They knew Gotti, but they didn't know what his visit meant. Thump rose from the table to face him.

"This how we do now?" Gotti quipped, suppressing his smirk.

"Nigguh, you lucky you still breathin'," Thump shot back, but it didn't come out as gruff as he usually was.

"Come on. I, I come in peace, yo. Give your boy the benefit of the doubt," Gotti replied.

Thump eyed him steadily for a moment, and then gave a slight nod. The gunman tucked his pistol.

"What you want, Gotti?"

"I need to holla at you."

"Holla."

"At *you*," Gotti repeated with emphasis on privacy.

"Let me holla at the nigguh," Thump said to the room. They cleared out. "You got a lotta nerve comin' here, yo."

"You know me, my balls, and my word." Gotti smirked.

"Well, you betta choose your words carefully, 'cause they gonna determine if you walk outta here. What the fuck was you thinkin' when you crossed me, nigguh?" Thump bassed.

"This shit ain't about you, Thump. You already know that. This shit about that bitch ass Love," Gotti bassed back.

Despite the fact that Thump agreed with the statement, he still spat, "Fuck you mean? You know if it's him, it's me, too."

Gotti shook his head with a disgusted chuckle.

"Still stickin' up for that nigguh when you *know* he ain't cut like that. Nigguh, *we* made that nigguh. *We* went hard while Love ain't do shit!"

"And I see you still on your bullshit, yo. Still in your feelings about that lawyer shit! But nigguh, we ain't flip on you. You flipped on *us!*" Thump reminded him.

"I flipped? How the fuck you figure? What you woulda done if the nigguh ain't even hold you down wit' a lawyer?"

"Gotti, I got you a lawyer!"

"But it was Love's charge! It was the fuckin' *principle!*" Gotti retorted thunderously.

Thump didn't respond right away, because he couldn't disagree. He thought back to that night three years back, when he and Gotti murdered a dude in his apartment. Gotti thought he heard their mark speaking to someone, but Thump urged him to leave because of the gunfire the neighbors might've heard. Neither of them realized there was a female hiding under the bed. That night ended with Gotti taking an unrelated gun charge for Love, but Love would later renege on getting Gotti a lawyer. At the time, Thump felt the same way as Gotti, but when Gotti came home and switched teams, that answered the question for Thump. Now they stood, two ex-partners, facing one another as enemies.

"Principle?" Thump echoed, closing the space between him and Gotti. "You talkin' about principles? You come home and ride wit' this bitch ass Swag, or whatever the fuck his name is, ridin' on *me,* and you talkin' about principles? Gotti, word up, get the fuck outta here before I—"

"I never brought it to you. That's why I'm comin' to you now. Put shit right between us. Fuck Love!" Gotti spat.

The only reason Thump didn't snuff Gotti on the spot is because he was beginning to feel the same way.

"Oh, what? I'm 'posed to be like you and flip on my man or somethin'?"

"That's your man, T? You sure? Huh?" Gotti questioned, the smirk on his face saying more than his words.

"Ay yo, Gotti. I ain't for your word games," Thump gritted.

Gotti pulled out his phone and hit speed dial.

"No words, yo. Just listen."

The phone was close enough that Thump could hear it ring, and then a voice said, "Yo."

Thump looked at Gotti.

Gotti extended the phone.

Thump took it.

"Who this?"

"You'll know in a minute, baby," Miss Toni replied, putting the phone on speaker and then putting it in his pocket.

Miss Toni had just pulled up to Love's club. It wasn't open yet, but the bodyguards were already on duty.

"Tell Love Miss Toni here to holla at him," he told the bodyguards.

"For what?" one of the bodyguards growled.

"You ain't lookin' nothin' like Love, shug. So umm . . . to the left please," Miss Toni sassed as he tried to pass.

The bodyguard blocked his path. "Hold up." He dialed a number, spoke, listened, hung up, and stepped aside.

"My name good as money, shug. Remember that," Miss Toni spat with an eye roll as he breezed by.

Once inside, various people were putting the final touches on the club.

Music played from the speakers, but not at full blast. Miss Toni looked up and saw Love standing at the floor to ceiling window watching him. Miss Toni took the VIP stairs and emerged a few moments later. Love was alone in the large room, propped up on the pool table.

"Where your man at? I was lookin' forward to meeting him face to face." Love smirked, but Miss Toni could see the anger behind it.

"He thought maybe me and you should talk first," Miss Toni replied.

"How we gonna do business if the nigguh scared to come see me?" Love quipped, thinking of the recent conversation he had, had with Swag.

"My offer still stands. We can make war or make money," Swag had said.

"And I still ain't interested," Love replied.

"Not even to talk?"

"Ay, yo. What you want, man?" Love questioned. "Why would you figure I'd want to talk to you?"

Swag chuckled.

"Let's talk about that."

Love finally relented, half out of curiosity and half out of pure interest. Love was pragmatic with his game. The bottom line was make money, but the longer he had beef, the hotter it got and the less money he made. Something had to give.

"Swag wanna make a deal," Miss Toni announced.

"What kind of deal?"

"One that'll keep, not your hands, but your numbers up," Miss Toni responded.

Love flexed his jaw muscle. Something he did when he was thinking. Miss Toni continued.

"Love, I've known you a long time. You've always been straight up when I dealt with you. You 'bout your paper, and you ain't for all that extra shit, so why not make a deal?"

"Because this nigguh killed my man," Love gritted, thinking of Antman. "Because he brought this bullshit to me! *That's* why!"

"Ant was a good dude, but with all due respect. This a dirty game, Love. You know that. So, what? You gonna let this stand in the way of why you in the game in the first place?" Miss Toni reasoned.

Love paced the floor.

"Look . . . even if I wanted to . . . make a deal. My nigguhs ain't gonna go for it. Them nigguhs want blood, and I respect that."

Miss Toni approached him.

"Even if that cost you everything? Swag go hard, and he ain't got nothin' to lose. You do. Regardless, it ain't your *nigguhs*. It's *one* nigguh, Thump."

Love stopped and looked at him.

Miss Toni smirked.

"We both know it's Thump that want blood, so it's Thump that's really standin' in the way of progress. So let me ask you this: If Thump *wasn't* around, then what?"

"Meaning?" Love questioned, even though he knew exactly what Miss Toni was saying.

Miss Toni smiled knowingly.

"Come on, Love. We both know you ain't no leak. Bottom line is, gettin' money, period. Anybody that get in the way of that . . ."

Love thought over the whole chessboard. He had a cop trying to extort him. That cop was Thump's girl. Was she a pawn for Thump or was Thump her pawn? And he had Swag, a nigguh he was beefing with offering to eliminate one problem . . . Thump. And maybe cause another one . . . the deal. But if he could use Swag like Jazmine wanted to use him, maybe he could play them off of one another. Love was a thinker. He thought he had the answer.

"Look. You tell your man. He solves my problem, we ain't got no problem."

Miss Toni nodded. "No problem then. Just give us the heads up on the nigguhs and it's done."

"Then it's done," Love confirmed.

Thump couldn't believe his ears. It was like watching your girl fucking another man, or hearing your brother rat you out to the police. He had just heard a nigguh he would've died for, plot to kill him. But his sickness was quickly replaced with a lava-like rage.

Gotti could tell by the look on his face that Swag's plan was working.

Thump handed him back the phone.

"Still think that's your man?" Gotti quipped.

Thump glared at him, but his anger was directed at Love.

"That nigguh think he can play me like that! He think he can play me like that!" Thump rumbled.

"I told you that nigguh Love ain't shit, T. Now you see it for yourself. Question is, how you gonna handle it?" Gotti taunted him.

"Fuck that nigguh! He wanna play dirty. We can play dirty, my word!"

"So what up, fam'? What you wanna do? I'm with you," Gotti assured him.

Thump stepped to him.

"I'ma take it to this nigguh's ass, yo! But I ain't makin' no deals wit' no fucking Swag! You fuck wit' me, then he go the same way as Love," Thump said, laying out the ultimatum.

Gotti shrugged.

"I'm for gettin' money, period. But if I can get it with family, all the better. Swag was just my way to get at Love," Gotti lied. He really did see Thump as family, but his lust for Swag was greater than his loyalty to the past.

"That's what it is then. We get rid of all these bitch nigguhs and link like real Gs!" Thump remarked, extending his hand for Gotti to shake.

They shook and gave each other a gangsta hug. Then Thump looked Gotti in the eyes.

"My word, Gotti . . . Don't cross me, man."

"Come on, nigguh. This Gotti you talkin' to, not Love."

# Chapter Twenty-Six

A s soon as Thump heard the knock on his back door, he cocked his .40 caliber and cautiously approached it. He could see a shadow against the brick wall that jutted out, separating his condo from the one next door and bracketed his back door.

"Yo, who dat?" he yelled.

"Me."

In that one word, he heard Jazmine's Georgia drawl, melted all over it, and he relaxed. He lowered the gun, but didn't tuck it. He opened the door, and Jazmine stepped out of night, shutting the door behind her.

"Yo, how the fuck Love know you are a cop?" Thump asked as soon as she stepped inside.

"He what!" Jazmine squealed, the surprise in her voice pitch perfect.

"The nigguh know you a cop."

"I can't believe this . . . but I'm not surprised." Jazmine shook her head. "This fuckin' asshole sergeant got me back on traffic duty, ridin' around givin' out fuckin' tickets! I'm lucky Love didn't kill me! What he say to you?"

"The nigguh came at me like I was a rat! Like I'm on your team! Fuck that. You on *my* team!" Thump bassed, hating to feel like his gangsta was being questioned.

Jazmine was quick to appease him and gas him at the same time.

"Baby, he know you far from a rat. He just showing the larceny he been had in his heart for you. If he'd flip on you that quick, he was never your man."

Her words brought the memory of Love's early treachery.

"So what's next?" she asked, as if she wasn't leading.

Thump looked at her. "The nigguh gonna try and kill me."

"Why you say that?"

He explained how Gotti had gone through and poured him a drink by allowing him to listen to Love's conversation.

Jazmine was speechless, but her mind was spinning in overdrive.

"Wow!" she intoned, adding, "Why didn't you tell me you had somebody in Swag's crew?"

Thump shrugged. "I thought the nigguh had just jumped the fence. I ain't expect him to come through like this."

"But baby, listen. You have to tell me *everything*. Maybe we could've been used that to get at Swag, you know!" Jazmine explained.

"True," Thump admitted, "but like I said, he had switched teams."

"Regardless, we can use this to our advantage." Jazmine smirked.

Thump caught on instantly.

"Ain't no goddamn way, yo! Ain't no way I'ma be a fuckin' sittin' duck! I know what this nigguh don't, and I'ma use *that* to my advantage!"

"Thump. Listen to me. I'm not saying be a sitting duck. I'm saying we can kill two birds with one stone. Get at Love *and* Swag at the same time! If he using Swag to get at you, then we *know* he gonna be there," Jazmine reasoned.

"But that don't mean Love gonna be there."

"He don't have to be. If we snatch Swag up, Swag will get us at Love!"

Thump thought about it a moment. He hated to admit it, but Jazmine had a point.

"Think about it, baby. If Love plotting on you, what makes you think he'll let you get close anyway? Evidently, Swag can. So Swag is our man." Jazmine summed it all up with a wink.

Thump chuckled. "I ain't know country girls played chess."

"Like my grandma used to say: Still waters run deep."

\* \* \* \* \* \*

Later that night, Miss Toni, Gotti, Swag, and Rain sat around the kitchen table playing bid whist. Miss Toni had just hung up the phone, and announced, "Love said Thump just called him. He wanna meet and talk things out."

Swag smiled greedily.

"Where?"

"The mall. Tomorrow afternoon," Miss Toni answered, picking up the cards and shuffling.

"If Thump said the mall, he doesn't trust Love. He pickin' a public place. That ain't Thump," Gotti warned.

Swag turned to him. "So what you think?"

"I think it's a set up. Thump smell somethin' fishy, so he gonna move on Love," Gotti surmised.

Miss Toni dealt the cards.

"That make sense." Swag nodded. "Shit, it'll be lovely if Thump murder Love, and we murder Thump. Talk about two birds with one stone, huh?"

"Malls mean beau-coup security," Miss Toni added, looking at his cards.

"No doubt," Rain agreed.

"So we got to get in and get out then," Swag replied, mind on one thousand. "Bottom line is this. We get who got. Feel me?"

"Huh?" Gotti grunted.

"He means we get at the nigguh slippin' the most. If it's Love, it's Love. If it's Thump, it's Thump. Both sides think we wit' them," Rain explained, because despite it all, she still understood Swag. At least she thought she did.

Swag looked at her with a smile. She rolled her eyes.

"Exactly," Swag confirmed, and then turned to Gotti. "Gotti, you take your team and lay on Love. Toni, you and your team lay on Thump. We catch as catch can."

Gotti and Miss Toni nodded.

Rain's phone rang. She answered, "Hello . . . naw. What's up wit' you? You already know . . . okay, gimme like a half hour . . . yeah." She hung up and started to get up from the table.

"Where you goin'?" Swag questioned.

"Out!" she shot back and walked out the kitchen.

Swag looked at Gotti. He shrugged. Swag got up and went behind Rain.

"What you mean out?"

"Just what I said," she replied sassily as she went in the bathroom. She tried to shut the door behind her, but Swag stopped the door from closing and stepped through it.

"Ay, yo, I know you ain't got a muthfucka comin' here," Swag said, seething with anger.

Rain looked him up and down.

"Do I look green? I don't want a nigguh knowin' where I lay my head no way. That's how you get stalkers," Rain replied, undressing.

Visibly relieved, Swag told her, "We still got this power move tomorrow."

"I'll be ready, but *trust*, I'ma get me tonight."

Rain stood before Swag totally naked, hands on her luscious hips, looking delicious.

Swag ran his eyes over her curves but didn't react.

Rain snorted.

"Hmph, just what I thought!" she spat. Rain turned on the shower, bending over in Swag's face.

When she felt Swag's tongue penetrate her pussy, she jumped and groaned.

"Sss . . . stop," Rain whined, but poked her ass out further. She wanted to pull away, and she hated the fact that her body so automatically reacted to his touch. Despite the circumstances, she still wanted him.

Swag slid two fingers in her pussy, twisting them as he pumped them in and out while his tongue worked that sensitive area between her pussy and her asshole. But when he slid his tongue in her ass, she gasped, "Oh fuck! Don't do that!"

He ran his tongue from asshole to clit, and by the time he began to suck, Rain came hard in his mouth. After her shivers, she got herself together. Rain straightened up, turned to Swag, and said, "Thanks for the nut, but I really have to get ready."

Swag couldn't help but laugh.

"Word? So I'm best for the head, huh?"

"We'll holla." Rain smirked, climbing in the shower and closing the curtain.

# Chapter Twenty-Seven

J azmine checked her watch, knowing she needed to hurry to get to the mall. She hung her uniform in her locker. Slammed and locked it and quickly headed for the door. Once she reached her car, she found Detective Maston leaning on it, arms crossed over his chest. She slowed her pace as she approached, readying her game face.

"How'd you do it?" he questioned.

"Do what?" Jazmine asked innocently.

He smiled, but she could see his rage beneath it.

"I'm going to admit that I underestimated you, but I promise you . . . I won't do it again."

"Detective, I have no idea what you're talking about." Jazmine still played the innocent role. She knew she had drawn first blood, so there was no need to flaunt it. "But umm, I really have somewhere to be, so . . ."

Maston uncrossed his arms and leaned off her car.

"Just wanted to let you know that we're *definitely* on the same page now, Coleman," he told her and then walked away.

\* \* \* \* \* \*

Love didn't want to be around when the bullets started flying, but he knew he had to be. He knew if Thump didn't see him, he'd think something was up. So Love had to play it all the way out.

"I'm here, yo. Where you at?" Love asked as he entered the mall.

"The food court," Thump answered.

"Cool. I'm on my way," Love confirmed, and then hung up.

Love had a couple of shooters on deck. He texted:

Love: *Food court*

Then he sent it to his shooters, Miss Toni and Swag.

Gotti saw the text and nodded to himself. He had three shooters with him. As he entered the mall through the underground parking lot, he had his game face on, knowing it was one shot, one kill, and he couldn't miss.

Thump checked his watch, and then carefully scanned the crowd. He saw his shooters planted around the food court. They were like pits, cold eyes glued on him waiting on the signal to kill.

"Fuck is this bitch at?" Thump growled to himself. He texted: *Where U?*

Jazmine saw the text and shot back: *I'm here.*

She was on her way up the escalator, stepping past people and climbing it like stairs. When she got to the top, she moved quickly in the opposite direction of the food court.

\* \* \* \* \* \*

Rain cruised the upper deck of the parking lot directly outside the food court as if she was looking for a park. But she was the backstop, in the likelihood that Thump made a break for the back door. She'd be waiting.

\* \* \* \* \* \*

Love moved toward the food court; his shooters on the opposite side of the walkway. People were so into themselves. No one asked why a few mall shoppers were wearing coats in the summer. Love turned the corner and the diverse smells of the food court filled his nostrils. He scanned the crowd and his eyes fell on Thump.

Thump saw Love as soon as he turned the corner. He couldn't believe it had come to this so easily between them. His mind flashed back to earlier times. High school. Broke. But things were simple then. When he saw Love stop and turn away, he knew had Gotti not pulled his coat he would never have thought Love would have set him up. But once Love stepped away, Thump made his move and his people let shit rip.

The split second before Love turned away, and he looked Thump in the eyes, he felt his soul shrink inside him. The one thing they had vowed, he had broken. Never to let anything come between them. But he had let a chick and money turn him against his oldest friend.

Now there was no turning back.

Thump's team opened fire first, a full second before Love's team bust.

The mall broke out in pandemonium, as if they were under attack from urban terrorists. People dashed, ducked, and screamed, but the bullets couldn't hear or see, so their protest was futile. Several bullets found innocent flesh, spilled bystander blood, and took the lives of those unfortunate enough to obstruct the ballistic's path.

But that was only the first wave.

Gotti and his team, coming up behind Thump's team two seconds later, opened up with a chorus of automatic fire hitting and killing one man of Thump's team. Even though all the shooters were wearing masks, Thump knew the tall one was Gotti just by the way he hid the automatic sideways when he fired. He wasn't surprised that Gotti had betrayed him so fast. Times had changed, and so had the game. As Thump dipped off, he vowed he would handle Gotti personally.

Outside, Jazmine had made it to the getaway van where two more shooters were waiting.

"You see her?" Jazmine questioned, as soon as she approached the van.

The passenger simply pointed to a car several rows away. Jazmine followed his finger and saw Rain waiting in the car.

"As soon as she make a move, I got her. Scoop us up ASAP, and then we'll scoop Thump and we out," she instructed.

The passenger, a man of few words, simply nodded.

Jazmine took a roundabout path to come up behind Rain's car. By the time she was a row over and began to duck walk to stay low, she could hear the muffled sounds of gunfire coming from inside.

"Shit!" Jazmine swore, hoping Rain didn't pull off before she could reach her.

She didn't.

Instead, when she saw Thump come bursting out of the door, Rain cocked her pistol and started to step out of the car. She could see that Thump thought he was home free. Rain started to raise the gun, but she felt cold steel to the back of her neck.

"Surprise, bitch," Jazmine gritted, "Guess who?"

Rain froze, expecting to breathe her last at any minute.

"You got me," Rain conceded, dropping her pistol.

The van skidded up. Thump jumped in, and then they skidded up in front of Rain's car. Jazmine gripped Rain by the ponytail, the gun to the base of her skull and pushed her inside the van.

"You get that nigguh!" Thump asked.

"No, but this bitch here gonna tell us or die for 'im!" Jazmine replied.

The van skidded off.

# ANGEL SANTOS

* * * * * *

If the first backhand from Thump dazed her, his second damn near knocked her out. If she hadn't been tied to the chair, she'd be asleep on the floor. But Rain's survival instincts were on overdrive, and she willed herself past the pain.

Jazmine sat on the table while Thump worked Rain over, and one of his shooters stood by the door smoking a cigarette.

"Oh, you a tough bitch, huh? That nigguh must be fuckin' you good to be holdin' him down like this," Thump remarked.

Jazmine hopped off the table.

"See, you playin' with this bitch," she spat as she snatched the cigarette out of the shooter's mouth.

She walked around behind Rain's chair, mashed her head forward, and ground the cigarette into the back of Rain's neck.

"Aaarggh!" Rain squealed. It felt like the cigarette had burned down to the bone.

"Just keep holding out and watch me get *real* creative!" Jazmine barked. "Now, where the fuck is Swag?"

"Fuck you and this black ass, cocked-eye nigguh! Y'all gonna kill me anyway, so I ain't tellin' you shit."

Jazmine laughed. "Damn, she gangsta."

"I'ma show you gangsta," Thump huffed, and then turned to his man and said, "Go get me a curlin' iron or somethin'."

Rain's stomach dropped when the dude left out the room, but she didn't let it show. Jazmine leaned down and whispered in Rain's ear.

"Woman to woman. Is that dick really good enough to die for?" she taunted.

"Fuck you!" Rain shot back.

The dude came bursting back through the door and handed Thump the curling iron.

"Ay yo, Thump. Duke just called and said Love hit the spot!"

"Fuck!" Thump barked. He turned to Jazmine and handed her the curling iron. "Make that bitch talk!"

Thump hurried out the door without waiting for an answer.

"Don't worry." Jazmine sneered as she plugged in the curling iron and eyed Rain. "She will."

Once she plugged it in, the red light glowed. Rain couldn't help but look at it.

Jazmine followed her eyes and chuckled.

"Yeah, I guess you know what that's for, huh? Helluva dildo that'll make."

Rain could just imagine the searing pain of having the burning hot metal being slid inside her pussy. Something in her wanted to just tell Jazmine where Swag was, but she just wasn't cut to rat. Her pedigree wouldn't allow her to.

"By the time it gets hot, if you ain't talkin', I'ma give you good dick," Jazmine threatened.

"Bitch, do you. But my hood ain't raise no rat," Rain spat back, gaining strength from her own words. She eyed Jazmine hard, remembering her face from that night at the club with Love. "I'm loyal, bitch. Somethin' I see you don't know shit about," Rain added.

Jazmine shrugged because she knew exactly what Rain meant.

"Oh, trust, I know all about loyalty . . . loyalty to me." Jazmine tested the curler. She snatched her finger back.

"Ssss hot." She brought it closer to Rain. "One more chance."

"Eat a dick!" Rain replied, but on the inside she was dizzy with fearful anticipation.

Jazmine laughed. "I like you. Therefore, I won't make this personal. Strictly business."

With that, Jazmine grabbed a handful of Rain's hair, jerked her head back, and then kissed her dead on the mouth. Rain took it as a kiss of death.

And it blew her mind.

# Chapter Twenty-Eight

J azmine glanced in the rearview mirror and smiled. Since Maston had let on that he had, had her followed, she stayed on point. She was well aware that she had been followed several times, but she had never tried to shake them. Of course, she didn't want to arouse suspicion. But today was different. Things were getting hot, and Jazmine knew it was time to tie a ribbon around the situation. So she drove another block and then turned into the parking lot of a large supermarket. She parked and made her way into the store. Jazmine knew the cop wouldn't follow her inside, and checking over her shoulder, she saw she was right.

She headed down the cereal aisle straight to the back aisle's meat section. Without breaking her stride, she went right through the plastic slats and entered the refrigerated section. The chill in the air put a pep in her step. The workers looked at her curiously.

"Lookin' for me, ma?" one worker flirted.

Jazmine smiled and winked, but kept it moving, straight to the back dock.

She hopped down, rounded the dumpster, hopped a fence and came out on the next block. In less than a minute, she had flagged a cab. As she rode off, she chuckled to herself, wondering how long the cop would sit uselessly in the parking lot.

* * * * * *

"You can't go in there!"

"Too late."

This exchange took place when Jazmine walked into Love's mentoring office, her old job. The new girl sitting in her old seat asked politely, "May I help you?"

"No," Jazmine replied without breaking her stride.

When she stepped to Love's office door, the girl said, "You can't go in there!"

"Too late," Jazmine answered as she stepped inside and closed the door behind her.

Love was sitting behind his desk on the phone with his gun on the desk in front of him. The girl burst in behind her.

"Love, I told her—" she blustered, but Love shook his head.

"Don't worry about it, Lisa. She good," Love told her as he hung up the phone.

The new girl, Lisa, gave Jazmine a dirty ass eye roll as she left and shut the door behind her.

"She's not as pretty as me." Jazmine shrugged.

As she approached the desk, she rounded it and then sat on it, right next to the gun. For a slight second, Love and Jazmine looked at the gun. She could tell Love wanted to move it, but he didn't want to show weakness, so he let it go.

"I think she is."

"Liar. Do you think about me when you're fucking her?"

Love snorted. "Ma, I ain't even think about *you* when I was fucking you," he shot back.

Jazmine laughed. "I like that. That was cute."

"You got somethin' to say, or you just came to waste my time?"

"Just that yesterday was a stupid move. Not even twenty-four hours and the governor is all over the city's ass," Jazmine explained, but she didn't have to, because Love already knew.

It was all over the news, Internet, and the newspaper. They were calling it a mall massacre even though only six people had died.

"And your point is?"

"My point is: Why didn't you come to me? I mean, we are partners . . . remember?" Jazmine reminded him with a taunting smirk.

"Come to you for what?"

"Thump," she replied, letting her tone of voice and facial expression convey exactly what she meant.

"Because, despite everything, him I trust. You, I don't," Love told her matter factly.

"Well, that's too bad. Because now you've made it where only *I* can get close enough to him so we can end this shit. So you may not trust me, but you gotta deal with me," Jazmine said coldly. Their gazes locked, silently assessing each other. Inadvertently, they both glanced at the gun.

"So what you saying? You gonna take care of Thump?"

"Just like you're gonna take care of taking me to your connect, *partner*."

"*We*, or should I say, *you* already made that deal."

"No, I mean today. Now," Jazmine insisted. "Pick up the phone, make the arrangements, and let's make it happen."

Love didn't budge.

"Either that, or I'm taking you in," Jazmine threatened.

Love laughed.

"Really? You and what army?"

This time when she looked at the gun, his look lingered on the glinting steel.

"Do it!" She smirked. "Pick it up. Do it."

He flexed his jaw muscles to temper his rising anger. "I don't like the smell of pine oil."

It took her a second to catch on that he was referring to the movie, *Training Day* when Denzel explained what death row smelled like. Then she laughed.

"I love a man that can make me laugh . . . Make the call."

He eyed her once more, and then slowly picked up the receiver.

\* \* \* \* \* \*

Gotti and Miss Toni lay in a post-coitus cuddle in his bed, while Luther Vandross woo-woo-wooed in the background and Gotti smoked a blunt.

"You love me?" Gotti questioned, after blowing out a stream of smoke.

"What you think?" Miss Toni answered.

"I ain't thinkin'. I'm askin, yo. Stop playin'," he gruffed.

Miss Toni lifted his head off Gotti's chest and looked at him.

"Boy, you know you my baby. You ain't shit, but I fuck wit' you too much to let that come between us."

Satisfied with the answer, the tenseness left his tone and he sucked on the blunt.

"I'm just sayin'. I just wanna know who you wit' if it come down to it."

"If what come down to it?" Miss Toni probed.

Gotti exhaled mist.

"Swag."

"Swag?"

"I'm just sayin'. I'm startin' to feel like this nigguh tryin' to play us, yo. It's been damn near a day, and we ain't heard shit from Rain! My cousin could be dead for all I know, and this nigguh ain't even givin' a fuck!" Gotti fumed.

Miss Toni sat up, hormone-induced titties swinging free.

"So what you sayin', Gotti?"

"I'm sayin' what I'm sayin'!" he gruffed. "Bottom line is Love 'posed to give you the connect, right?"

"Yeah."

"That's how Swag set it up, right?"

"Yeah."

"Why you think he did it like that? 'Cause he wanna front you off! Make you the face and keep me and my goons for his Do-boy Army! Fuck that shit!"

Gotti was heated. It wasn't just Rain, really. It wasn't Rain at all.

The problem was lust unquenched. He wanted to fuck Swag so bad, but Swag kept taunting him, teasing him, never giving completely in, so that Gotti's lust had become frustration. Frustration had become anger, and anger had become greed for Gotti. If he couldn't get some, he wanted it all.

Miss Toni listened to Gotti's rant and had thoughts of his own. He had pondered why Swag had set the deal with Love to go through him. But unlike Gotti, he knew it was a method to Swag's madness. He may have wanted Swag to fuck him, but the bottom line was Miss Toni saw Swag's game was tight, so he didn't catch feelings. But he knew he had to appease Gotti.

"I hear you, baby. Let's just let the shit play out, you know?"

"Yeah, but if shit hit the fan, who you wit'?"

"You already know." Miss Toni smirked.

\* \* \* \* \* \*

Twenty minutes after Love made the call, he and Jazmine pulled up to a soul food restaurant named Kingfish. It was a family style place with an area for dining and an area for takeout as well. The place was moderately packed when they walked in and made their way through the rows of tables to the back. The smell of smothered pork chops and collared greens wafted through the air.

"Smells like home." Jazmine giggled.

Love didn't comment. They bypassed the kitchen and headed down the back hall to the last door. Love knocked.

"Yeah," came the muffled invite from inside.

They entered to find a big fat black man that favored Cedric the Entertainer sitting behind the desk, eating from an enormous plate of fried chicken and biscuits and gravy.

"My man, Love. What's going on?" Kingfish greeted with a mouthful of food. His eyes looked Jazmine over, but he was more interested in the chicken.

"Kingfish, how you, unc?"

"Good, good. Have some?" Kingfish offered politely.

Love held up his hands. "I'm good."

"How 'bout you, miss lady?"

Jazmine smiled. "No thank you."

Kingfish grunted and went back to eating. Love sat down on the outer edge of Kingfish's desk while Jazmine leaned against the wall, folding her arms across her breasts.

"You know you need to cut back on all that fried food," Love remarked with a smirk. "You know you old."

Kingfish sucked a bone clean, snorted, and then dropped the greasy bone.

"Nigguh, if I wanted medical advice, I'd go to the doctor," Kingfish shot back, only half joking. He licked his fingers, and then wiped them on a napkin. He nodded at Jazmine.

"This her?"

Love glanced at Jazmine with a neutral glare. "Yeah, it's her. Jaz, meet Kingfish."

"How are you? I would shake your hand, but I'm scared to get in the way," she joked.

Kingfish chuckled lightly and leaned back in the chair.

"From what Love here tells me, you ain't much afraid of nothing. What you up to takes hella balls. Where you keep yours?"

Jazmine laughed. "In the back of my panty drawer, but for this, I don't need 'em! What I'm doin' is best for all of us."

"What makes you so sure?" Kingfish quizzed.

"The only reason I became a cop is because the best way to break the law, is make the law. Now, I'm sure a man like you can appreciate that, and with me playing my position, Love's hands stay clean. And you don't have to worry about dealing with his void and the bullshit that comes with who's gonna take his place," she explained deftly.

Kingfish tented his fingers and nodded.

"Lil mama, I've been doin' this probably before you was born, so what makes you think I need your help with any bullshit?"

Amused, Love looked at her as he awaited her reply. Jazmine came off the wall, approached the desk, and leaned her weight on her palms.

"Because you have two options. Kill me now, or deal with me later. With all due respect, I don't want to be a problem for you, but please believe me. You *don't* want to be a problem for me. Within a year, I'll have the narc division in my back pocket. That alone is worth its weight in gold. Believe me. With me, we all eat,  but without me—shit will get very, very ugly."

She stood up straight.

Kingfish was silent for a moment, and then he quipped, "Decatur?"

Jazmine smiled. She knew the deal was made. The tension disappeared.

"Naw, Savannah. Born and raised."

Kingfish shrugged.

"Hell, I was close. I'm hell when it comes to accents. I'm from Athens myself. I like you, lil' mama. So I'm inclined to give you a chance . . . *one* . . . chance," Kingfish emphasized, holding up a massive index finger.

"That's all I need." She winked.

Kingfish leaned back into his meal.

"Now, y'all get the hell out my office and let me eat," he gruffed mildly.

Love slid off the edge of the desk.

"And stay away from that pork," Love cracked.

Kingfish waved him off.

As Love and Jazmine crossed the parking lot to the car, Love mentally assessed the situation. He may not have liked the way Jazmine muscled her way into the situation; he couldn't deny that the picture she painted made sense. With Thump out of the way, his last connect to the street would be cut, giving him a new face to show for his move into politics. On top of that, with Jazmine holding him down in the police department, he'd not only have the mayor, but the police in his pocket! The thought made him chuckle and sparked a related thought.

"What's so funny?" Jazmine asked.

They stopped at the trunk of the car.

"I can't front, ma. You go hard in the paint. I'ma start callin' you the maestro."

Jazmine giggled.

"I just know what I want, and I know how to get it."

"No doubt. And on the real, this shit could definitely work for the both of us. But you gonna need somebody on them streets that go just as hard," Love suggested.

"Who you got in mind?" She probed.

SWAG

Instead of answering, Love pulled out his phone and hit a number. A couple of rings later, he heard, "Yeah."

"Ay, yo. Toni . . . Meet me at my club ASAP."

* * * * * *

Thirty minutes later, while Jazmine and Love played pool in his VIP office, Miss Toni was escorted in by one of Love's goons, who left as soon as he let him in.

Miss Toni approached the table, eyeing Jazmine curiously.

"Where I know you from?"

Jazmine shrugged.

"Maybe I gave you a ticket. I'm a cop."

"Cop?" Miss Toni echoed indignantly, and then looked at Love. "Love, what the fuck kind of shit you into?"

Love chuckled. "Yo, chill yo. This my people, Jaz. Jaz, this Miss Toni."

"Hello, Miss Toni. How you doin'?" Jaz greeted.

Miss Toni looked at Love and then back at Jazmine.

"So what's this all about?" Miss Toni wanted to know.

"Shug, trust me. You've got nothing to worry about. I'm on your side," Jazmine assured him.

"And what side you think I'm on?"

Jazmine smiled.

"Gettin' money. Gettin' rid of Thump. I provide the protection, and you run the streets. You interested?"

Miss Toni looked at Jazmine, sizing her up. He switched his weight from one foot to another.

"I'm listenin'."

Jazmine laid her cue on the table and approached Miss Toni.

"Like I told Love, y'all fucked up trying to hit Thump in the mall. Now, I'm the only one that can get close to him, and I will. With him out the way, we can put the guns up and get money. That is, if you're willing to do your part."

"Which is?"

"Give us Swag," Jazmine replied.

Miss Toni smirked.

"Funny, Gotti was just talkin' about that same thang."

Jazmine smiled, ironically.

"Then we should be on the same page."

Miss Toni shrugged.

"Maybe, but personally, I fuck wit' Swag. The nigguh go hard. Besides, I don't move like that and cross my people. But if Gotti go at him, then I ain't got nothin' to do wit' that, 'cause Gotti my people too."

"I respect that. Hopefully, you'll see me as your people one day."

"Play fair and I will."

Jazmine nodded. "So if Gotti go at Swag, you won't get in the way?"

"Naw."

Jazmine looked at Love. "Then you need to holla at Gotti."

Love nodded.

Jazmine extended her hand to Miss Toni, who took it and shook it.

"Welcome to the team." Jazmine smirked.

# Chapter Twenty-Nine

B aby, please! Don't let them kill me!" Rain cried into the phone on the other end. Swag stood in Gotti's living room while Gotti sat on the arm of the couch watching him.

"Ma, calm down, okay? We got you. My word. You not gonna die," Swag assured her.

"Please . . ." She sobbed.

"Just put Thump on the phone," Swag instructed her.

"Who the fuck is this?" He frowned. "Jaz? Who the fuck is Jaz?" Swag growled. Then he looked at Gotti with a questioning look.

Gotti just shrugged.

"Bitch, put Thump on the fuckin' phone! You laugh like it's a game, but I promise you I'll laugh last. Yeah . . . yeah . . . How I know you ain't gonna kill her anyway? . . . Okay, listen, bitch. If you cross me, I'll . . . Hello? Hello?" Swag pulled the phone from his ear, and then he looked at Gotti.

"Who the fuck is Jaz?" Gotti questioned.

"I don't know, but evidently she carry weight 'cause she speakin' for Thump."

"What up with Rain?" Gotti probed, concern coloring his tone.

Swag sighed.

"Yo, G. You already know how this shit go. Just because we play our part don't mean they play theirs."

"What the fuck they want?"

Swag looked him in the eyes and said, "You."

"Me!" Gotti echoed, standing up.

Swag nodded.

"That nigguh Thump feel a way about you crossin' him. Bottom line is, it's either you or Rain."

Gotti shook his head and started pacing the room.

"Man, goddamn!" Gotti growled in anguish. "Yo, Rain like my sister. What the fuck!"

Swag watched him agonize over the decision, and then said, "Listen, yo. Tell me something. Real talk."

Gotti turned and looked at him.

"What?"

Swag approached him. "You feelin' me? Like that?"

"What's that got to do—"

"Just answer the question."

"I'm sayin' . . . I don't know. You play too many games, yo."

Swag nodded. "Yo, I know. Believe me, G. That ain't me. But *this* ain't me. I ain't never felt no dude. Naw, I ain't gonna lie. I ain't never felt no dude *like this*. This shit new to me. But one hunnid. I'm feelin' you like crazy and I got mad love for Rain. In a way, I feel this shit on me too, yo. Thump might want you, but I'ma give 'im me."

Gotti looked at him, unable to believe what he was hearing.

"What you mean 'give him you'?"

"They want us to meet them. The way I see it, if we can show them you, but once we make the switch, it's me, then we got a chance to save Rain because we make the switch at the same time."

Gotti deflated, shook his head.

# S W A G

"It'll never work."

"It's all we got. Once we got Rain, then whatever happens, happens. I got my trusty friend," Swag said, mustering a smile and patting his bulletproof vest. "So maybe I can make it out. Besides, I killed his man, Ant. That should be enough to make him forget you."

Gotti couldn't believe his ears.

"You'd do that for me?"

Swag looked him in the eyes and said, "I'ma real nigguh, yo. I go hard for mine, and the way I feel about you, you definitely mine. If I make it out of this, you got my word. No more games. It'll be me and you."

Gotti felt love and guilt. Love, because someone was really willing to die for him, and guilt because this was someone he was ready to kill! He didn't know how to answer in words, so instead he pulled Swag close and tongued him passionately.

After the kiss that left him with a hard dick, Gotti said, sincerely, "I love you."

"I love you, too."

\* \* \* \* \* \*

"On the strength that I knew your baby father, God bless the dead. If your people play fair, I'ma play fair. But if not, bitch, you dead," Thump warned, looking Rain dead in the eyes.

She knew he was telling the truth.

"They play fair."

"You better hope so. Put her in the van," Thump ordered his two goons.

They were the only goons left of his squad. The ones that weren't dead or got shook and fell back, had crossed over to Love when the beef split the crew. They took Rain to the van. Thump jumped on the phone and hit Jazmine.

"Yo, where you at?" he questioned as soon as she picked up.

"Where I'm 'posed to be, baby," she assured him. "I'm at the spot she said they rest at, but I don't see nothin'."

"You think she lied?"

"Naw, she wanna live. I just think they probably relocated just in case she broke down," Jazmine surmised.

Thump nodded. "Then I think we should change the meeting spot."

"That makes sense. I'll call 'em and let 'em know once you ready."

"Yep."

They hung up.

* * * * * *

Swag came from behind their building to the back parking lot where Gotti was waiting. He climbed in the car.

"Yo, I know that was that bitch Jazmine!"

"Where?"

"She was layin' on the spot for like ten minutes, but she just pulled off, yo. Rain had to have told her where we rest," Swag surmised regretfully.

Gotti shook his head and squeezed his eyes shut tightly.

"Damn, yo. They musta tortured her hard body, yo. You think she dead?"

Swag thought about it, and then answered, "Naw, I doubt it. She might be fucked up, but she ain't dead."

Swag got on the phone. "Yo, Toni."

"Yeah."

"Spot blown. You go 'head to the meetin' spot," Swag instructed her.

"'Kay."

They hung up.

Swag looked at Gotti.

"Go wit' Toni to the spot. I'ma come behind you. Make sure this bitch ain't slick, ai'ight?"

"Yeah, man," Gotti replied, looking irritated and worried.

"Yo, don't worry. We good," Swag assured him and then popped out the car.

Ten minutes later, Swag hit Gotti.

"Yo."

"That bitch just hit me. They changin' spots. They wanna meet at the cemetery now," Swag told him.

"That's a fuckin' setup!"

Swag chuckled. "Yeah, but we the one doin' the settin'. She tried to be slick and laid on our spot up the block. I peeped her. Right now I'm followin' her! So don't sweat it. Go to the cemetery and wait for my call."

Gotti laughed.

"Yo, I can't front. You're a sharp muthafucka."

"You already know."

*Click.*

* * * * * *

Thump pulled up to the spot in the cemetery where he was supposed to meet Jazmine. He and his goons got out of the van, one dragging along Rain. Everybody was tense, guns drawn, heads on swivel. Thump checked his watch.

"Fuck she at?" he mumbled, pulling out his phone and hitting Jazmine's number.

Several rings, no answer. He texted: *Where you at?*

Still no response. Thump thought about the fact that she had gone to Swag's rest to try to track him. Could anything have happened? The thought sent a chill through him. He couldn't lie, he was truly feeling Jazmine. Not only that. She was as sharp as a tack. But it wasn't like her to not hit right back.

"Stay on point," Thump told his goons.

"You already know," the one holding Rain replied, jamming the gun more firmly to her side.

There was something about a cemetery at night that made people think thoughts they wouldn't otherwise think. It amplified sound and sometimes played with your vision. Jazmine knew that. That's why she suggested the spot. Call it a psychological advantage.

Thump's phone vibrated with a text: *At the crypt*

Her message brought Thump a sense of relief, but he was still irked that she didn't answer right away-right away. Her text had told him she was at the meeting place, on the other side of the cemetery.

"Let's go!" Thump instructed.

There was little light except the occasional lamppost. The closest one was a few yards away, which made the trees cast long shadows as they walked in between them. The only sounds were the sounds of their own footsteps and the rustle of expended breath.

As they neared the lamppost, they had to step through a pair of trees. After Thump passed, a few steps later, all he heard was two gunshots that went off almost simultaneously. He spun around ready to blaze, but found himself face to face with the infrared beam centered on his forehead. Both his goons lay brainless and twitching on the ground, and Swag held Rain and the gun.

Swag had laid on them as they past the trees. As soon as the goons were in striking distance, Swag stepped from behind the trees and shot them both point blank in the back of the head. Now Thump stood all alone, gun only half raised, faced with the ultimate decision. Go out blazing, or try to live another day. He chose the latter.

"Take your chances, or drop it, but do it *now*." Swag seethed with anger.

# SWAG

Thump, sizing up the situation, let the gun fall from his hand, and then raised them slowly.

"You got it, champ. Where's Jaz?"

Swag smiled.

"In the right place. This a cemetery, ain't it? Get his gun, ma."

Rain walked over and picked up Thump's gun, and then aimed it at him.

Swag walked in a wide arc around Thump and stood under the lamppost.

"Gotti!" Swag yelled out.

Several seconds later, Gotti and Miss Toni walked out of the shadows, guns aimed at Thump.

"What's up, homey? Lookin' for me?" Gotti laughed, eyeing Thump.

Thump flexed his jaw.

"Nigguh, whateva' happen, you still a fake ass nigguh."

"Word? Yeah, fake this!" Gotti barked, but right before he squeezed the trigger, another gun went off.

Swag's.

But he didn't shoot Thump. He shot Gotti, blowing out his knee. Thump's jaw dropped. Miss Toni's eyes bulged, and Gotti wreathed in agony on the ground.

"What the fuck are you doin'!" Gotti screamed. "You shot me!"

With cold eyes, Swag looked at him and replied, "Exactly."

Miss Toni pointed his gun at Swag, and instantly, Rain put her gun to Miss Toni's head.

"Bitch, what is you doin'? This muthafucka just shot your cousin!"

"Stay out of it, Toni. Remember? You're neutral," Swag said, looking at him. "Now put it down."

Feeling Rain's steel at his temple, Miss Toni reluctantly covered his weapon. Rain took it out of his hand with the situation under control. Swag tucked one gun and lowered the other.

"Now that I've got everybody's attention." Swag chuckled. He looked down at Gotti holding his knee, blood oozing out from between his fingers.

"How's your knee, baby?"

"Fuck you! What the fuck is goin' on?" Gotti questioned, in total confusion.

Swag laughed.

"That's what you wanted, huh? You really wanted to fuck me. Guess I fucked you, huh?"

Swag approached Thump.

"You loved that bitch, didn't you?"

He didn't say a word, but he didn't have to. It had been written all over his face.

"What hurt more? Me killin' her, or your man, Ant? That bitch ass nigguh screamed when that fire hit him."

A tear rolled down Thump's cheek. It wasn't from weakness. He wanted to break Swag's neck so bad he could taste it.

"But like all good things, this too must come to an end. So, game over."

Swag stepped back a few feet. Thump expected in that next moment to be dead. Instead, Swag laughed and pulled off his glued on mustache and goatee.

"What the fuck!" Gotti gasped.

"*You* . . ." Thump rumbled with total confusion in his tone.

Miss Toni got it instantly and couldn't help but break out laughing.

"Ain't no goddamn way!" Miss Toni cackled.

Jazmine was Swag.

"Damn that shit hurt comin' off," Jazmine said, rubbing her chin. She looked at Gotti and then Thump. "I guess I got some explaining to do, huh?" she said, her southern drawl gone, replaced with a thick New Orleans accent. She pulled her fake eyebrows off to reveal her perfectly arched real ones. Then she took out her green contacts and discarded them in the darkness, revealing her true hazel gaze.

"You a bitch?" Gotti quizzed in total disbelief. The revelation almost made him forget the pain in his blown knee.

"Just make sure you smile when you say it," Jazmine retorted.

"It was you . . . the whole time," Thump hissed, feeling like someone had punched him in the gut. Not only had he loved the enemy, but she had killed his man and broke up his crew. He was sick.

"Goddamn!" Miss Toni gasped.

Rain simply smiled. She had known ever since that night she was being held hostage and Jazmine had kissed her. The kiss that blew her mind. There she was being kissed by a girl but tasting Swag! Her eyes bulged and she had snatched away.

"What the fuck! Who?" Rain had sputtered.

Jazmine threw her head back with laughter, and then in Swag's voice replied, "You already know."

Right then Jazmine told her everything. When she finished, it finally hit Rain and took all the wind out her sail.

"What about . . ." Rain signified, and then looked at Jazmine's crotch.

Jazmine laughed. "A strap-on, ma. An extremely uncomfortable strap on."

"I can't believe this . . . I'm in love . . . with a woman?"

Rain couldn't believe it. She thought she knew herself, but despite it all, despite the fact that she now knew the truth, nothing had changed. She still loved Swag.

"Don't worry, ma," Jazmine had cooed, kissing her gently. "This woman loves you too," she lied.

Now, in the cemetery with her mask totally shed, Jazmine pulled the other pistol from her waist.

"I want you two to think back . . . three years ago. When the two of you ran up in an apartment and murdered my man," she began, holding back the tears that she had suppressed for so long. "'Member that? 'Member that?" she asked them both. "I loved him just like I made you love me. I loved him . . . I loved him so much I *became* him. I *breathed* him!" Jazmine emphasized. She looked to the sky and yelled, "This is for you, baby."

With that, she raised both guns and let them blaze simultaneously, blowing Thump off his feet and twisting Gotti in two different directions. She emptied the clip in both of them.

When she was done, tears streaming down her cheeks, the sound of gunshots still echoing in her ears, she turned and walked up to Miss Toni.

"The only reason you alive is because you pulled my coat to Gotti, and you played fair. Now, I still wanna fuck wit' you. You still wanna fuck wit' me?"

Miss Toni laughed.

"Fuck wit' you? Bitch, I wanna *be* you!"

Jazmine smiled tightly through her tears. She looked at Rain.

"Baby, y'all get it outta here. I'll catch up. I got one more stop to make," Jazmine informed them, and they both knew what she meant.

Rain winked.

"Okay, daddy."

# Chapter Thirty

A s Jazmine approached the door of Love's club, the bouncer stepped in her path. She flashed her badge without breaking stride and breezed inside.

Once in, she glanced up at Love's glass panelled VIP office and saw him standing at the glass like a man on top of the world. Despite the crowd, he saw her come in. Their eyes met and stayed locked until she disappeared into the staircase that led to his office. Once more she was blocked, and once more she flashed her badge. The bouncer stepped aside and she ascended the stairs. When she got to the top, she found the door open, and Love waiting for her.

Jazmine stepped through the door and eyed Love silently.

"Ay, yo. Let me holla at shorty for a minute," he told the five dudes in the office.

They left, closing the door behind them. Jazmine approached the desk.

"So?" he asked.

"Didn't I tell you I'd take care of it?" Jazmine quipped, a hint of mockery in her eyes.

A sense of relief passed through Love. He had won.

"So what you drinkin'? We celebratin'." Love chuckled.

Jazmine didn't crack a smile or take her eyes off him.

"Nothing."

Love scowled. "What's wrong with you?"

Jazmine silently savored the moment and then announced, "The police are on the way."

"The police? I thought you were the police?" he joked, but his gut told him this was no joke.

"They think that you may resist arrest—that because I tracked you here after you killed Thump, that you might—use the gun on me, leaving me no choice," she said in a calm but ominous voice.

Love's senses went on full alert.

"Ma, what the hell are you talkin' about?" Love quizzed

He tried to slide his hand under the edge of the desk.

Jazmine took her left hand out of her pocket, revealing the revolver in her palm. She cocked the hammer.

"Don't do that," she warned him, calmly but firmly.

He raised his hands, mocking, and then rested them both on the desk.

"Oh, so you want it all, huh? You can't run this shit without me!" Love smirked arrogantly. Even though deep down, he knew he didn't have any cards left to play.

Before Jazmine could answer, they heard the music stop and commanding barks that only police make. Love got up from the desk and looked down at the club. Police were everywhere.

"You stinkin' bitch!"

Jazmine didn't respond. She pulled her phone out and called Love. His phone rang on his desk and then rang again. Love looked at her.

"Go ahead. Answer it."

Love snatched it off the desk and put it to his ear.

"Ay, yo," Jazmine said in her Swag voice. This is for Gaws."

# SWAG

As soon as Love heard the voice, but saw that it was coming out of her mouth, it all came together, the whole setup. Like when your life passes before your eyes.

"God . . . damn!" Love sighed, seeing she had caught him totally slipping. *Gaws* . . . Then he remembered sending Gotti and Thump to New Orleans to assassinate Gaws, who stood in the way of his expansion into NOLA territory. Love's message had been heard loud and clear. Especially by the woman hiding beneath the bed, who had heard her man being murdered in cold blood.

Jazmine lifted the gun and fired into Love's chest five times, the force of the shots throwing him back and through the plate glass window.

Just as his body fell three stories and landed on the bar, the police burst into the office and trained their guns on Jazmine.

"Freeze! Don't move!"

"Relax. I made the call. I'm a cop," she announced nonchalantly, and then held up her badge.

Seeing the badge, the three officers relaxed and holstered their weapons.

Jazmine made her way around the desk and looked down on Love's body sprawled on the bar. His eyes were still open and seemed to be looking at her.

One officer stepped up beside her and looked down.

"What happened?"

Jazmine looked at him, shrugged, and replied, "I thought he had a gun."

That would become the official story.

She walked out.

# Chapter Thirty-One

*Three weeks later...*

As the mayor-elect of this great city, it is an honor to be able to announce today that we have truly turned a dark page. The infamous Love Organization is no more!" Joyner said, as he stood on the steps of city hall.

The small crowd before him was made up mostly of the press with a few TV cameras sprinkled throughout. Behind him stood the Chief of Police, Detective Maston, and Jazmine in full uniform.

"If it wasn't for the brave work of Chief Jordan, Detective Maston, and Officer Coleman, our city would still be under siege. So it is with great pleasure that I thank them, and on behalf of the entire force, courtesy of Chief Jordan, I present Officer Coleman with her detective shield."

A smattering of applause broke out from the crowd as Jazmine stepped to the microphone. Joyner handed her the badge. They posed for a picture with Jazmine holding up the badge, and then they shook hands and Joyner stepped back.

"Thank you, mayor-elect Joyner, and I look forward to working with you in keeping this city clean." She smiled, glancing at Joyner. Their exchanged gaze conveyed the inside joke they shared. "And I also thank Chief Jordan for giving me the opportunity to do my part. But the biggest thanks goes to Detective Maston. If it wasn't for the detective believing in me and keeping me undercover, this would've never happened. So detective, thank you," Jazmine gushed, turning her head to look at Matson. She smiled politely, but his eyes stayed serious and avoided her gaze.

"And . . . I hope, soon-to-be Chief Detective of Narcotics, Maston." She snickered. "Again, thank you."

As she stepped away from the microphone, the press began firing off questions. Chief Jordan stepped to the microphone to field them.

Jazmine shook hands with her partner in crime, mayor-elect Joyner.

"Maybe I should call you the mayor," he quipped, half joking.

Jazmine winked. "Naw, you look much better in the spotlight."

As she moved away from Joyner, she almost ran into Maston. She could tell he had been waiting for this moment. The two adversaries eyed each other steadily. His gaze stern, while hers secure in her victory, returned his indulgently.

"No hard feelings, chief?" She smiled, offering her hand.

He looked at it, and then back at her. Finally, reluctantly, he shook it. He knew she had set off the incident that had sullied his name and jeopardized his chance of becoming chief narcotics detective. Then, by shining up to Chief Jordan that it was Maston who masterminded the whole operation, helped put his name right back at the top of the list.

Maston knew she would be a formidable opponent.

"You probably think I owe you," Maston said, giving her a cold smile. "You're right. I do," he added.

Jazmine knew the debt he was referring to was retribution. She nodded.

"Have it your way." She started to walk away.

"Coleman!" he called her.

She turned back.

"You look kinda sick. You okay?"

Her thoughts turned to Hall and how she had played him. She knew exactly what he was getting at. She turned and walked away.

Jazmine walked around the corner into a small parking lot and headed toward Miss Toni's Escalade. She hopped in the backseat. Miss Toni sat behind the wheel, and Rain sat in the passenger seat.

Rain looked at Jazmine.

"Kingfish just called. He said he ready when we are."

"Ai'ight."

Rain smiled and shook her head admiringly.

"Yeah, you definitely got swag."

Jazmine laughed. In her Swag voice she replied, "You already know, ma. Now let's get this gwop."

The three of them laughed as Miss Toni pulled out into traffic.


- T h e   E n d -

# Swag Reading Group
## Discussion Questions

1.      When you originally read the title Swag, what did you think the book would be about? Explain.

2.      Do you believe there was another way Jazmine could have earned a higher position on the police force instead of sleeping with Detective Hall? Explain.

3.      Who was your favorite character? Least favorite? Why?

4.      Consider Jazmine's job as a police officer. Are women just as proficient at working in male dominated fields such as law enforcement? Why or why not?

5.      What message or theme did you get from the book?

6.      What were your thoughts when you discovered Jazmine and Swag were one and the same person?

7.      Consider Love and Thump's friendship. Should Jazmine have been so successful at destroying the male bond they had, had since childhood? Why or why not?

8.      Rain, Thump, Love, and Gotti all fell for Jasmine whether she was being herself or Swag. Were they all in lust or love? What are your thoughts about love and lust?

9. Was Love too ambitious? Or was he doing the right thing by trying to make an exit from the dope game? Explain your answer.

10. Should Thump have killed Jazmine the moment he found out she was a cop? Why or why not?

11. If you were the author, would you have written any scene differently? Explain your answer.

12. Should Rain and Ms. Toni have remained loyal to Gotti? Why or why not?

13. Was Jazmine justified in killing Detective Hall? Explain.

14. Rain originally suspected Swag wasn't completely on the up and up. Should you always trust your gut feelings? Why or why not?

15. Was the end satisfying? Please explain your answer.

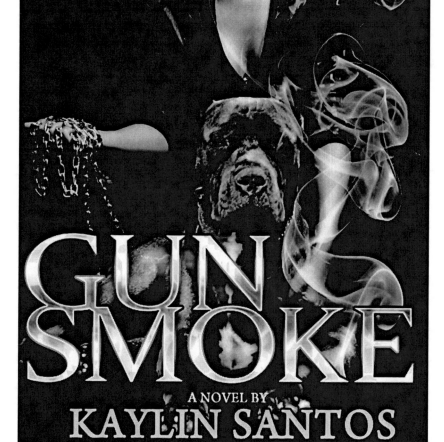

# WAHIDA CLARK PRESENTS

# GUN SMOKE

### A NOVEL BY
# KAYLIN SANTOS

# Chapter 1

D og fights and gambling went hand and hand at Lauryn's spot. She sat at the mini bar entertaining one of her high rollers who had been upstairs gambling for six hours straight before coming up for air. It was typical for Lauryn, to also be the host some nights at her small time casino. She really didn't mind hosting, nor did she mind all the attention her 38 DD breasts got either, just as long as those puppies kept niggas wanting to gamble at her place.

"We got a problem," Simair whispered to Lauryn as she poured the high roller another drink.

Lauryn quickly got up and followed Simair toward the basement where the lights were dim, and the sound of barking dogs filled the air. When she made her way down the steps, she noticed only one dog in the dog ring, and a small crowd stood behind Mark, the owner of the dog. Normally, there would be two dogfights per day in her establishment, but today there wasn't one person trying to put their dog up against Mark's dog, Busta. "What's goin' on down here?" she asked nonchalantly as she stepped into the ring.

"Don't nobody wanna fight," Mark shot back in an aggressive tone. He looked over at the two would-be dogfighters who backed out after seeing what they were up against. "I got 10K that my dog will kill anything that steps in this ring."

Lauryn looked shocked and even chuckled at the amount of money that Mark was willing to bet on his dog. The average dogfighter wouldn't bet any less than 15K per fight, of which 10% of the winnings would go to the house. She scanned the room and calculated the potential side bets before determining that she would entertain this wager, along with any other bets that rode with Busta.

She stepped out of the ring and walked toward the back where she slid open a door that was cut off from the rest of the basement. Lying there on a mattress was Lady, a red nose pit bull who was in the middle of nursing her puppies. Lauryn didn't have to say a word as Lady rose to her feet, wagging her tail, happy to see her owner. Side by side, they both walked to the ring with one thing on their mind . . . kill!

"Fuck am I supposed to do with this?" Mark asked, looking at the playful, frail female dog as she jumped into the ring.

"What? You said nobody wants to fight. I'll see ya 10K and I'll take all side bets!" Lauryn yelled out to the spectators. "Fight to the death! Round one. No clock. Being as though you got a male dog, there's no odds. Straight bets," Lauryn announced.

Mark thought Lauryn was crazy, but he acted fast in pulling out the 10K and passed it over to her. He knew there had to be something special about Lady, but he decided to go with his gut instinct. *There is no way in hell that Busta's gonna lose this fight,* he thought.

Lauryn pulled her long black hair into a ponytail, kneeled down and gave Lady a kiss on the top of her head. Simair began collecting money from the side bettors, and within a minute, the ring was clear and the fight was ready to begin.

Busta stood there barking and pulling at the chain that held him back. Lady just sat there looking confused and scared, with her tail tucked between her legs as though she wanted nothing else but to get out of the ring. Standing in front of her petite-sized owner, didn't make Lady look too convincing either.

# GUN SMOKE

A motion from Lauryn to Mark signaling him to let his dog off the leash was all it took. Within the blink of an eye, Busta was all over Lady, and had locked onto the back of her neck with jaw-crushing force.

Lauryn looked on without saying a word. While Mark, on the other hand, continued to yell out, "Kill! Kill!"

*"Defensa!"* Lauryn spoke to Lady in Spanish, calmly telling her to defend her neck.

Lady quickly gave Busta her back, and the tail that was tucked between her legs sprang out and began to wag. Busta continued shaking the back of Lady's neck, refusing to unlock his grip.

Mark looked over at Lauryn with victory in his eyes, but was confused by the giggles that she and Simair shared while looking down at the two dogs.

Lady was only toying around with Busta, and her wagging tail showed her playfulness. But playtime was over. Lauryn knew that Lady was a little weak from nursing her puppies and had to end the fight quickly.

*"Castigado!"* Lauryn said. *Pierna! Pierna!"* she instructed Lady to punish Busta.

Lady immediately got low to the ground and went for Busta's two front legs. Busta tried to tuck in both of his legs, but only saved one. Lady bit down on the other one, forcing him to loosen his grip on her neck, which was all she needed.

*"Huevos!"* Lauryn finally yelled out, seeing an opening.

In one swift jolt, Lady released Busta's leg, darted up under his body, and locked onto his balls. The agonizing pain shot through Busta's body so sharply that he never thought twice about trying to bite back. He howled at the top of his lungs, and his cries echoed throughout the basement.

Hearing the word, *"Matalo!"* spoken by her master, Lady knew that meant "kill". She yanked and yanked at Busta's balls until the skin started to break.

The bystanders grabbed a hold of their own nuts and turned away, knowing what was about to happen next.

Lady yanked until she ripped his balls off, and when she did, she dropped them on the floor and went right back for Busta's dick.

That was enough. Mark couldn't take anymore. He pulled a .38 snub nose from his back pocket, aimed it at Busta and pulled the trigger. But he didn't stop there. He kept squeezing the trigger, striking Lady in her head in the process. By the time he emptied the revolver, Lauryn and Simair were aiming a pair of twin Glock .40's at his head. Not only was Mark out of pocket, but he was also out of bullets.

It was one thing to fire off shots in the casino, but it was a whole other ballpark killing the only true friend that Lauryn had outside of her family. Her mind was racing, and all she wanted to do was blow Mark's head off. For a second she pictured his brains splattered all over the spectators behind him. Her desire to kill him was suppressed by the the kind of heat a dead body in the basement of an illegal casino would bring; not to mention the many witnesses looking on.

Lauryn lowered her gun, but Simair was reluctant to do the same. He was unwilling to let Mark leave the basement. "Clean dis shit up and get dis dickhead out of here!" Lauryn said as she lowered Simair's gun. "Basement's closed!" she announced to the spectators.

Lauryn looked down at Lady one last time before turning around and walking up the basement steps, holding back the tears filling her eyes.

# GUN SMOKE

Mark stood there with a stupid look on his face, regretting what he had just done. He knew beyond a shadow of doubt that this wasn't going to be the end of this situation.

# WAHIDA CLARK PRESENTS

A NOVEL BY

## TASHA MACKLIN

# *Chapter* 1

# 1999

"Stop that shit before it be a problem," the menacing bully threatened as Dre beat his pencil against his desk in an agitated manner.

Dre peered at the oversized bully and the clock on the wall. "Three minutes left on the last day of school and you wanna take a beat down home with you for the summer," the guy known as Big Mike said.

"What?" Dre replied with a frown.

Everyone in the classroom, including the teacher, shifted their eyes toward the bully with the pair of arms that bulged from his crisp white T-shirt.

"This is a class and it"s almost over," the teacher said. "But it is possible to get expelled on the last day of school."

Dre"s eyes still beamed at the bulky looking dude, sizing his opponent up. Big Mike outweighed Dre"s tall, lanky body by fifty pounds and his frame was as twice as thick. Images of the last two people the beast had knocked out flashed in his mind.

Big Mike tucked his gold chain in his T-shirt. "I"m getting left back again, so I don"t give a fuck about being expelled. I might fuck around and drop out." 28 x3 y5 over 7x7p + 16 x5 y3 over 14y5

"Or get *knocked out*," Dre said, masking the fact he was leery about fighting.

# TASHA MACKLIN

The bully smirked, looking at Dre"s dusty Air Force ones. "Bum ass nigga," he spat, glaring at Dre. Then he turned to the class and started cracking jokes about Dre"s clothes. "Look at his dusty ass shoes. This nigga wearin" biscuits. Broke, bum ass!"

"All right, this is not a comedy club," the teacher said, gazing at Big Mike condescendingly.

Dre was furious. He grinded his teeth, tightening his jaw while quickly tapping his right foot. It wasn"t the first time his impoverished upbringing had become a distraction for him striving to make his way in the streets of Detroit.

The bell rang and the class began dispersing. Dre stood as the bully winked and began cracking his knuckles. As Dre took a step behind the bully, his teacher stopped him. "What"s up, Ms. G?" he huffed.

"You"ve got a brain, so use it," she said.

"Sometime you have to act off of street smarts," Dre replied, glaring at the Big Mike"s back.

"There are plenty of youth who thought like that. You know where they are now?"

Dre shrugged his shoulders.

"Cells and caskets. There"s never a shortage of prisons."

Dre shook his head, thinking of his mother being murdered on the streets and his father being in prison. "Can I go now?"

"You still planning on going to college for computer programming? Your math scores are impeccable."

"I don"t know," Dre said. His love of numbers was dwindling, with the exception of counting money. Going to college would be a pricey bill on his back that would only worsen his financial strain.

"Don"t throw your life away, Dre." The teacher pointed at his head. "Use it." She stepped from in front of him."

2

He walked off, happy to be finished with high school and the teacher trying to run his life. If Ms. G was genuinely concerned, she would try and do something to help him and his grandmother overcome poverty. Dre stepped out of class, his eyes roaming the hallway in search of the bully. He elbowed his way through a throng of students who slowed his motion to put school behind him. His sneakers beat against the dark waxed floor as he heard someone call out his name. Dre slowed down and peeped over his shoulder in the direction of the voice.

"I know you weren't planning on breaking out without me," his best friend Nut said, walking through the crowded hall with the confident swagger of a young gangster. The lit Black and Mild dangling from his mouth was proof of how little he cared about school or rules.

Dre smiled and gave his man a pound. As he embraced Nut, he could smell a slight stench emanating from him and assumed Nut hadn"t taken a shower. *Damn, his old girl must have let the water get turned off again. He could have taken a shower at my spot.* "I wasn't trying to leave you, nigga. I just ain't used to you being here in the damn first place." Dre shook his head at the foolish scowl Nut wore.

"Pssst . . . whatever, nigga. I'm here now, so let's bounce," Nut said, exhaling a cloud of smoke and walking off to lead the way.

"I got beef," Dre said, staring at Nut.

"What?"

Dre hesitated in telling Nut about the bully, because he knew Nut was going to ride for him. Although Dre wanted to handle his drama alone, he knew he would need help.

"Just point the motherfucker out and we giving it to him!"

Dre looked at the demented sparkle in Nut"s eyes. *Damn, I got his crazy ass ready to go in*, Dre thought.

# TASHA MACKLIN

\* \* \*

"Where the fuck this clown ass nigga at?" Nut asked, looking around the chaotic scene around them. People scurried in all directions in an attempt to leave the school grounds by any means.

"I don't know." Dre stood on the stairs in search of his target. Students rushed toward waiting buses and filled them up quickly. Used and new cars pulled up and took off after eager students jumped inside. Twice Dre spotted his dream car, wishing he had a whip parked in the lot, so he and Nut could ride out. Although Dre was used to walking, he was ready to ride in many ways.

"You still don't see that nigga?" Nut asked.

Naw. I still don't know—" Dre's words were cut short by a wild haymaker that collided with his cheek.

Big Mike got off a second sucker punch from behind before Nut landed two quick blows to his jaw.

"Bitch ass nigga!" Dre barked as he followed up with a punch that knocked the bully down the steps.

Nut's foot came crashing down on Big Mike's head and face without remorse. Within seconds he was bloody, and a circle of students had formed around the assault.

"The principal coming!" one of the students yelled.

Dre looked up, noticing the principal in the distance. "Come on!" He grabbed Nut's arm.

"Fuck that!" Nut said, jumping in the air and crashing both his feet down on the bully's face, leaving him unconscious. He continued stomping him.

"We gotta *go!*" Dre shouted, pulling Nut as the principal closed in on them. They ran off through the crowd, leaving the bully with blood dripping down his face and splattered on his white T-shirt.

"Motherfuckers gonna respect us!" Nut declared.

4

# BALLER DREAMS

Dre wanted the respect Nut spoke of, but he knew that in addition to issuing out beat downs, it would take money to earn respect on the streets.

*  *  *

Dre was halfway through the next block when he noticed a hottie he had been checking for since he was a freshman. "Come on, man," he said, hitting Nut before making haste to catch up to the pretty girl on the move. He picked up his pace and searched for some surefire game worthy of him spitting at her. Ducking through the small crowd, he found himself a few feet away from the gorgeous brown-skinned honey. "Tagier," he called out as he darted behind her, catching her attention just as she stepped off the curb.

Somewhat surprised that he had called her name, Tagier glanced over her shoulder at her boyfriend Dante, who was engaged in a cell phone conversation. The last thing she needed was for him to catch her talking to another nigga. Seeing he was busy, she returned her gaze to Dre as he made his way toward her. She had to admit that his appearance embodied perfection. Tall, slim, with some of the longest, silky braids she had ever seen on a nigga. Those characteristics, along with his flawless brown complexion enticed her.

Dre reached Tagier before he could come up with any lines worthy of using.

"Umm . . . I've been seeing you a lot in traffic for a while now and . . . I . . . um . . . was kind of wondering if maybe we could get together or something," he stuttered, eyeing her short, curvaceous frame.

"I can't, Dre. I'm sorry, but my boyfriend wouldn't like that," she replied with downcast eyes.

As Dre opened his mouth to respond, his words were cut short by the loud outburst indirectly meant to disrespect him.

5

"Tagier, get your ass over here and I don't plan to say it again!" the angry voice blared.

He shifted his eyes from Tagier to the candy painted purple Impala and glaring jewelry of the individual with the ice grill. Tagier nervously jumped at the sound of the command. "I have to go, Dre. That's my man." She turned to leave and then added, "I guess I'll see you in traffic."

Dre watched her sexy frame as she hurried across the street. He couldn't help thinking that it had to be a big, bear-looking nigga's money that had Tagier speeding away from him. She looked too good to be with an ugly nigga. Dre returned the mean glare Dante shot at him. But Dre's jaw dropped when dude's hand connected with the side of her face. Tagier dropped to his feet in shock and a plea for help in her eyes.

"Faggot ass nigga like to hit women!" Dre exclaimed in anger, stepping from the curb on some save-a-ho shit.

"Yo, what you doing kid?" Nut asked, following Dre. "Let that nigga discipline his bitch."

Dre wanted to smack the smug grin off the punk nigga's face. The bear-of-a-man pulled a silver revolver from his waist and pointed in Dre and Nut's direction, angering Dre more as he and his friend stopped.

"No the fuck he didn't!" Nut blared. "That nigga done lost his damn mind."

Dre was silent, engaging the man with an unwavering stare. The thug was far more dangerous than the bully Dre and Nut had just pounded out. So Dre knew his position in relation to him, and therefore, he held his composure as Dante yanked Tagier by the hair and tossed her in the car. The humorous look he gave Dre as he got in the car and pulled off infuriated Dre more. Dre knew if he and Nut were on top of their game, Tagier would be his and no one would have dared pull a tool on them. At that moment, Dre made up his mind that shit was gonna change. He was tired of being just another nigga in Motor City, and he was determined to become someone who would demand respect by any means.

* * *

Dre's mind went into overdrive as he and Nut reached their neighborhood. He had been silent, plotting their next move. To take things to the level he desired would require deep thought and an intricate plan. But Dre had always been a thinker.

Dre and Nut came upon a crowd huddled around a dice game at the corner of their block. Nut jumped into the game, tossing money on the ground and taunting a gambler. "You got something on ten or four, nigga? I'll gladly give you six and eight."

Dre continued walking and scanned the block in a wide sweeping motion. His mind flipped crazily in an attempt to formulate a plan. Then he realized that throughout the years his neighborhood had virtually remained the same. The faces had changed, but his block still held the reputation as one of the country's most prosperous dope strips. It was sad, but Dre had no doubt that the same street he stood on would fuel his rise to power.

The harsh reality of his environment reminded him of his father, who was serving time in a federal prison. Dre experienced a slight tinge of doubt. He had always imagined his father's suffering over the last ten years. The man now imprisoned had become a legend on the same streets his son stood on contemplating an identical lifestyle that could land him in prison.

Dre sighed at the realization of what he had to look forward to if he failed. He took a closer look around him, summing up the scene once more. Crackheads and dope fiends lined the block, while rats paraded through the trash strewn about the

7

multitude of burned-out lots. Dre laughed to himself to ward off the sadness of the situation. But ironically, he loved his neighborhood, regardless of how disheveled its condition. It was the only home he had ever known.

"What up, doe? Holler at your nigga, baby," Jamal said, snapping Dre out of his thoughts.

Dre was immediately reminded of what he loved most about his hood: his niggas. "What up, Jamal?" he responded, thinking that his dog walked, talked, and generally carried it as raw as any Eastsider he knew.

"You know me, baby. I'm just trying to make moves and stack this cheddar," Jamal said, staring up the block.

"Yeah, I feel you. With all these pipeheads running around, cheddar shouldn't be too hard to stack at all."

"That's exactly why I'm out here on the prowl." Jamal grinned. "Have either of my cousins been through here, playboy?"

Even as big as Jamal's family was, Dre didn't have to guess which of his cousins he spoke of. Nut, Gaines, and Jamal were the tightest out of the family. "I just left Nut up the block at a crap game. I haven't seen Gaines though."

"Cool. I'll catch up with you later." Jamal gave Dre a pound before heading up the block.

Dre began walking home, thinking of his own business plans. Succeed or fail, he knew his grandmother would be there for him. Just the thought of the woman who had raised him and given him everything within her means softened his heart. His love for her was indescribable, and he had never done anything to hurt her. She was all he had, and as much as he hated to admit it, his decision to hit the streets would crush her.

Dre wanted to turn away from his block as he reached home, spotting the dilapidated buildings and debris strewn around. He held his breath as the stench of trash dumped in the yard of an abandoned house hit him. Everything he was experiencing on his simple trek home told him he had to act soon to change his living conditions. He leaped up the steps of his house and made it inside.

"Grandma, I'm home," he yelled, heading upstairs.

"I'm in the kitchen," she responded in her usual jovial voice. "Come here, baby."

Dre stopped, backpedaled down the stairs and strolled into the kitchen. The sweet aroma resonating from the oven enticed his nostrils. He gave his grandmother a kiss on the cheek. "What's that in there smelling so good?"

She grabbed a dishtowel and nonchalantly replied, "Oh, it's nothing but some ribs, macaroni and cheese, deviled eggs and some homemade buttered biscuits." She began wiping the counter. "Why you ask? You hungry, boy?"

"You already know I am, lady." Dre quickly reached for the oven door.

"Oh, no you don't. Get out of my food and wash your hands, John, Jr. You know better than that."

As his grandmother began preparing a plate for him, Dre dragged his tall, lanky frame to the sink. It dawned on him that no one but her called him by his government name. He grinned at the thought and then wiped his hands on the dishtowel and reached for his plate.

"I'm so proud of you, John, Jr. Graduating in the midst of all the things you've had to deal with on a daily basis in this poverty ridden neighborhood is no small feat. For you to have stayed focused and never fallen victim to the streets like your father makes me a very happy woman." She reached out to hug him. "Enjoy your meal, baby. I love you."

Dre was tongue tied as he embraced her. After letting her go, he watched her head to the door. Right before she opened

it, she turned to him and said, "Ford, Chrysler, or General Motors will be honored to give you a job. But if you decide to go to college I'll gladly find a way to scrounge up the money." She strolled proudly out of the kitchen with a smile.

Dre plopped down at the kitchen table. No longer hungry, he pushed his plate aside, thinking about the truth in his grandmother's statement. One of the Big Three would gladly hire him if all he aspired to do was work on an assembly line making cars like thousands of other Detroit natives. But that wasn't the life Dre had in mind. He needed to control his own destiny, even at the risk of hurting the woman who cared for him more than anyone. Dre had only one life to live and he was going to live it to the fullest, no matter who tried to stop him at home or on the streets.

**THIS IS THE ORDER THAT WAHIDA'S BOOKS
SHOULD BE READ:**

THUGS AND THE WOMEN WHO LOVE THEM
EVERY THUG NEEDS A LADY
THUG MATRIMONY
THUG LOVIN'
THE GOLDEN HUSTLA
JUSTIFY MY THUG
WHAT'S REALLY HOOD
PAYBACK IS A MUTHA
PAYBACK WITH YA LIFE
PAYBACK AIN'T ENOUGH
SLEEPING WITH THE ENEMY

**CHECK OUT TITLES BY
WAHIDA CLARK PRESENTS PUBLISHING**
TRUST NO MAN 1, 2 & 3 BY CASH
THIRSTY 1 & 2 BY MIKE SANDERS
THE GAME OF DECEPTION
BY VICTOR L. MARTIN
NUDE AWAKENING BY VICTOR L. MARTIN
KARMA WITH A VENGEANCE
BY TASH HAWTHORNE

KARMA: FOR THE LOVE OF MONEY
By TASH HAWTHORNE
THE PUSSY TRAP 1& 2 By Ne Ne CAPRI
LICKIN' LICENSE 1 & 2 By INTELLIGENT ALLAH
THE ULTIMATE SACRIFICE By ANTHONY FIELDS
THE ULTIMATE SACRIFICE: LOVE IS PAIN
By ANTHONY FIELDS
FEENIN' By SERENITI HALL
STILL FEENIN' By SERENITI HALL
A LIFE FOR A LIFE 1& 2 BY MIKE JEFFRIES


**TITLES FOR YOUNG ADULTS**
THE BOY IS MINE! By CHARMAINE WHITE
PLAYER HATER By CHARMAINE WHITE
UNDER PRESSURE By RASHAWN HUGHES
NINETY-NINE PROBLEMS
By GLORIA-DOTSON LEWIS
SADE'S SECRET BY SPARKLE


WWW.WCLARKPUBLISHING.COM

WAHIDA CLARK PRESENTS

# FLIPPIN'
# *Hustle*

A Novel by
## TRAE MACKLIN

National Best Selling Author
WAHIDA CLARK

Eleven Novels...
11 Years later..

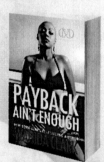
PAYBACK
AIN'T ENOUGH

ON SALE
NOW

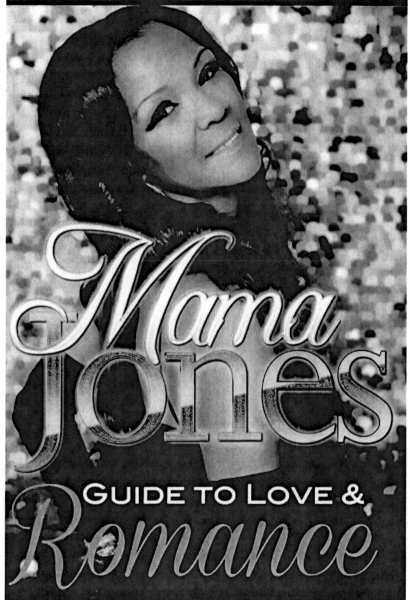

WAHIDA CLARK PRESENTS

# Mama Jones
## Guide to Love &
# Romance

New York Times Bestselling Author of Justify My Thug
CASH MONEY CONTENT
Honor Thy Thug
WAHIDA CLARK

WAHIDA CLARK PRESENTS

# The Devil's GAME

A NOVEL

SHAWN 'JIHAD' TRUMP

CPSIA information can be obtained at www.ICGtesting.com
Printed in the USA
LVOW10s1747210915

455070LV00001B/192/P